Nick stretched out a hand to clasp hers

"Natalie?" His face came nearer, and she shrank away from him until there was nowhere to retreat on the lounger. "Whatever happened to my lovely, warm, impulsive seventeen year old?"

"She grew up, became cool and sensible—and intends to remain that way," Natalie said levelly. "You can hardly expect people to keep their emotions on ice until some juncture more suitable for you , Nicholas Marlowe." She pulled her hand away from his.

Nick sprang to his feet, stooping to pick her up bodily from the lounger. He held her there for a moment, then lowered her abruptly to the grass and lay with half of his body on top of hers. He looked deep into the smoldering eyes so close to his own.

"It's no use, Nat," he said caressingly. "I've got you just where I want you."

CATHERINE GEORGE
is also the author of this
Harlequin Romance

2535—RELUCTANT PARAGON

This book may be available at your local bookseller.

For a free catalog listing all titles currently available,
send your name and address to:

HARLEQUIN READER SERVICE
1440 South Priest Drive, Tempe, AZ 85281
Canadian address: Stratford, Ontario N5A 6W2

Dream of Midsummer

Catherine George

Harlequin Books

TORONTO • NEW YORK • LONDON
AMSTERDAM • PARIS • SYDNEY • HAMBURG
STOCKHOLM • ATHENS • TOKYO • MILAN

Original hardcover edition published in 1983
by Mills & Boon Limited

ISBN 0-373-02571-8

Harlequin Romance first edition September 1983

CHAPTER ONE

NATALIE was late. Breathlessly she pushed and dodged through the crowded Heathrow terminal, a smile and murmured thanks magically gaining a path through the arrivals lounge as travellers of every nationality and colour gave way to the vivid urgency of the tall, graceful girl.

A great many eyes, mostly male, watched admiringly in her wake as Natalie Ross moved swiftly towards her goal, the arrivals barrier at Terminal Three. Her eye-catching mane of curling bronze hair was caught at the nape of her neck with a silk scarf in the same glowing shade of amber as her plain shirtwaister dress, the severity of the style throwing into relief her opaque, creamy skin, glowing with health, a beguiling spatter of pale gold freckles across the bridge of her short, straight nose. Long, slightly tilted brown eyes lit with the warmth of her wide smile as a tall, camera-strewn man in a ten-gallon hat made courteous way for her, almost causing her to miss the man who was waiting with ill-concealed impatience at the barrier. Natalie caught sight of him and her face lit up as she waved vigorously to attract his attention.

At that distance he was unmistakable. Edward Herrick's sleek, perfectly groomed dark hair, his discreet silk tie, the pristine white collar and lightweight suit, remarkably free of creases despite a seven-hour flight, were all so characteristic of his personality Natalie smiled fondly as she reached him.

'Edward!'

The man swung round at the sound of the husky voice, a smile in his narrow grey eyes, pointedly ignoring several envious male glances as Natalie flew towards him, hands outstretched in welcome. He clasped them gently and kissed her briefly on the cheek, putting her away from him as he picked up his holdall.

5

'Hello, Natalie, how are you?'

'I'm fine, darling, sorry I'm a bit late.' She took his arm, hugging it to her as they made their way towards the exit. 'The traffic was heavy and you were through Customs much faster than I'd calculated.'

'They didn't stop me, presumably as I just had hand luggage. Where's the car?'

'Second floor of the indoor car park; it's quite hot outside. Not that it will be anything to you after the burning desert and all that. What was Qatar like? Did you enjoy it out there? How did you cope with the heat. . . .'

'One thing at a time,' interrupted Edward patiently, as they made for the car park. 'It's a very interesting place, quite flat, of course, just a tongue of desert projecting into the Arabian Gulf, really.'

'Do you want to drive, Edward?' Natalie offered him her keys as they reached the car.

'No, thanks. I'd better take time to readjust to the left-hand side of the road again.' He smiled in apology and settled himself in the passenger seat of the little yellow Mini. 'Driving out there can be a bit hair-raising, as a matter of fact. Every roundabout's like tackling the first fence of the Grand National; nothing about giving way to the right, though to be quite accurate I suppose it would be to the left.'

'That can't have pleased you very much!' Natalie grinned mischievously at him as she guided the car towards the tunnel leading from the airport, and headed for the M4 and Chiswick. It was a beautiful warm June day, and they were heading for London just as the rush-hour was beginning to make itself felt. 'Did you have much social life?'

'People were very kind.' A slightly constrained note crept into Edward's clipped, very Establishment voice. 'I was entertained rather a lot, of course. There's very little to do if not invited out. Contrary to my previous impression it actually is possible for a foreigner to drink alcohol out there, as they're allowed a monthly liquor quota, but of course there are no public bars.'

'Were you able to swim at all?'

'Happily, yes, most days in fact. When the temperature is forty-five degrees even a swim in warm sea water is refreshing.'

'Darling, will you hand me the sunglasses under the dash, I'm a bit glare-conscious,' asked Natalie, 'though it's our own gentle British sunlight.'

'Restful, though I find I quite enjoy the heat, actually. It certainly doesn't bother the Qataris; do you know they actually play Rugby, and there's a national soccer team too, with a Brazilian manager and trainers. The support is fanatical. . . .'

Warming to his theme, Edward went on regaling Natalie with facts and figures about Qatar until they were within reach of the Chiswick fly-over.

'Goodness, Edward, you sound like an encyclopaedia; you certainly learned a lot about the country in a month,' commented Natalie, feeling somewhat battered by the amount of information flowing over her.

'Always best to familiarise oneself with new places.' Edward stretched out in his seat as far as the small car allowed, yawning hugely, a long slender hand in front of his mouth. 'That's quite a long hop from Bahrain, actually, especially with the shuttle-flight from Doha thrown in. I think it's beginning to catch up on me.'

'Would you prefer to go straight to your place?' asked Natalie immediately. 'I'd prepared a meal at the flat, but nothing that won't keep. If you're tired . . .'

'No, no of course. Besides, we have a lot to talk about.'

Nevertheless, Natalie's earlier glow of anticipation dimmed a little, and as she turned off the M4 and headed into Chiswick she was troubled by a nebulous feeling of disquiet. They were soon in the road of big old three-storey houses where Natalie shared a first-floor flat with Margaret Ryan, a staff nurse at Charing Cross Hospital.

'Where's the redoubtable Maggie today?' asked Edward drily, as he followed Natalie into the quiet flat. He deposited his bag with a sigh of relief and sank on to the sofa.

'She's not off duty until eight, at which time she is

tactfully going to an air-conditioned cinema with one of the ever-attentive housemen.' Natalie smiled saucily and sat beside him. 'I won't give you her reasons word for word. Suffice it to say she thought we'd like the evening alone together.'

For some reason Edward and Maggie, a vivid, blue-eyed brunette from Dublin, most definitely did not hit it off.

Natalie sat for a moment, looking at the recumbent man alongside her expectantly, then she leaned over him, looking down into his cool grey eyes, her own alight with mischievous invitation.

'I know you don't like demonstrations of affection in public places, darling, but we're quite alone now – aren't you going to kiss me properly? Or even a little improperly, if you like, it's been a long time.'

Edward reached up for her obediently and kissed her as instructed, but when Natalie would have prolonged the kiss he relaxed his hold and sat upright, leaving her no alternative but to do the same.

Brushing back his hair, he smiled apologetically.

'Actually, Natalie, I'm devilish thirsty, and I think you said something about a meal? The food on the plane didn't appeal very much, I'm afraid.'

Experiencing a distinct feeling of rebuff, Natalie rose promptly, smiling brightly to disguise her hurt.

'Of course, Edward. The usual?'

She went through into the little yellow and white kitchen and measured a double gin and a large quantity of tonic into a tall glass, added ice and lemon and took it back to him, pausing a moment automatically while he tasted it.

'Perfect.' Edward sighed with satisfaction, a look of content settling on his narrow, clever face as he stretched out, legs extended before him, in the nearest thing to a sprawl he ever allowed himself. He opened one eye and looked up at her standing there in silence.

'Aren't you having one? By the way, I like your dress; never go in for anything frilly, do you? Of course, with your height that's probably very wise.'

He subsided into inertia again.

Natalie bit her lip, keeping calm with effort.

'I bought it in Harrod's sale. If that was a compliment, thank you,' she said tartly. 'I'll just start heating the casserole. Practically everything's prepared in advance, so it won't take long. It's your favourite, Boeuf Bourgignon.'

'Splendid,' he answered somnolently, 'I'll just close my eyes for a moment.'

Natalie turned on her heel with just the hint of a flounce and went back to the kitchen to turn on the burner under the bright red casserole. Something's wrong, she thought, measuring and frying rice in a smaller matching pot. Her mind went round in circles, endlessly speculating on the reason for Edward's strangely lukewarm attitude as she added boiling stock to the rice, turned down the heat and put the lid on tightly. Mechanically she sliced mushrooms, sauteeing them gently with pearl onions, adding a little white wine filched from the bottle ready to drink with the meal. She put sweetcorn to heat in melted butter, filled a pan with water to boil ready to pop in frozen petits pois at the last moment. No dessert, of course, Edward disliked sweet things, so Natalie carefully arranged a board with a selection of cheeses, including his favourite Brie, and a crystal tumbler filled with stalks of crisp celery.

So maybe Edward and I *don't* have a sizzlingly passionate relationship, Natalie thought uneasily, her hands moving independently of her preoccupied mind. This suits me, and apparently him, very well, or at least it has until now. But after a month's absence—and presumably abstinence—it wouldn't be unreasonable to expect something of a fairly physical sort of reunion, surely. This morning there I was, tearing round preparing the food, fussing over which dress to wear, totally motivated by the prospect of Edward's arrival, with a few girlish thoughts of his arms round me and at least a kiss or two, not to mention impassioned assurances of how much he'd missed me. And there he is, reclining languidly on my settee, showing rather more enthusiasm for a gin and tonic than for good old Natalie.

She scolded herself irritably. There could be all sorts of reasons for Edward's lack of—enthusiasm? Jet lag, overwork, hunger. Yes, that was it, she decided, he needed feeding, and she transferred the cooked vegetables rapidly to serving dishes and put them in the warm oven with the plates. She took two wooden bowls of salad from the fridge and carried them through to the living-room, where a small round table was already laid for two by the large window.

'It's ready, Edward.' she said briskly.

The slim figure rose in one graceful movement, and Edward surveyed the table with pleasure, inspecting with almost greedy satisfaction the crisp salads, garnished with white chunks of crab and succulent pink prawns.

'This looks delicious—full marks, Natalie.' He sat down and shook out his napkin.

I wasn't sitting an exam, she thought, nettled, then smiled at his evident relish as he set to.

'Was the food good out there?'

'Oh yes; anything one likes, at a price, of course. Luxury consumable goods are imported, although the Qataris have a considerable food production programme. They certainly work hard for their future.'

Natalie had barely made a pretence of picking at her salad when Edward laid down his knife and fork, his plate clean. She half rose, but he put out a hand.

'Wait a while. There's something I must tell you before we go any further.'

'Yes,' Natalie's voice was flat, 'I rather thought there was.'

Edward refilled their wine glasses before speaking, and Natalie clutched hers with both hands as though it contained some miracle panacea for whatever ill was about to befall her.

The man opposite her was silent for a while, looking down at his clasped hands. Natalie's nerves were stretched to breaking point by the time he spoke.

'Natalie,' Edward said finally, his eyes looking directly into hers, 'there's no easy way of saying it. I've been milling over this all the way from Doha, and I really can't think of a better way than to be blunt. To be brief, I met someone else out there and I'm marrying her in a month's time.'

Natalie sat like Lot's wife, motionless, her eyes fixed on his in disbelief, all the healthy glow fading from her face, leaving her with such a translucent pallor that Edward grew apprehensive.

'I say, you're not going to faint or anything, are you?'

She took a deep unsteady breath and smiled very faintly, then drained her glass of wine, taking time to refill it before answering.

'No, Edward, I'm not going to faint—or anything. I just feel somewhat poleaxed, that's all. After all, you may remember that I had this odd notion you were going to marry *me*, though I must confess that Christmas was the earliest I could pin you down. She must be quite a girl.'

He looked at her in obvious discomfort.

'I wish there were some way I could justify myself, Natalie, but there isn't. I met Lisa at the first party I was invited to in Doha, and that was it. For both of us. We were introduced to each other and instantly everyone else ceased to exist. It was agony tearing myself away from her to come back to the U.K.'

Natalie winced, but Edward went on relentlessly.

'In fact, I've come back only to give in my reports to the firm, and to tie up a few loose ends. Then I'm going back to head up the Engineering Department in Doha. Lisa and her parents are arriving next week, the wedding will be a week later, by special licence, then we've planned a honeymoon in Cyprus on our way back to Qatar.' He reached across the table and took her hand, which lay flaccid in his like a dead thing. 'I wish it hadn't been necessary to hurt you, Natalie, but you're such a well-balanced, sensible person, completely level-headed; I know you'll accept this gracefully.'

Natalie regarded him with strangely detached wonder, then finished her glass of wine, refilling it with what remained in the bottle.

'Is she pretty?' she said dully, 'and young?'

She watched with sick fascination as Edward's eyes

took on a glazed hot expression, as though he were looking inward at a mental picture of the girl.

Natalie felt a shudder of angry distaste at the frankly sensual expression on his normally rather ascetic face.

'She's utterly fantastic,' he said, his voice thick with remembered excitement, the look on his face that of a schoolboy with his first crush, rather than the image of sophisticate he normally took great care to project. 'Red-gold hair, bright blue eyes, a figure to take your breath away, though she's only just over five feet tall—makes one feel very protective. And of course, she's only twenty.'

Rising to her full five feet ten inches, weighed down by every minute of her twenty-four years, Natalie took the salad bowls into the kitchen and switched off the oven. Then she collected a bottle of Burgundy which had been getting itself up to room temperature on the counter, opened it with a herculean yank of the corkscrew and took it back into the living room to refill her glass.

'You don't care for red wine, I know, Edward,' she stated categorically, 'now do go on.'

Edward looked towards the kitchen expectantly.

'Will the next course be long?'

Natalie's eyes widened in mournful reproach.

'How can you think of eating at a time like this, Edward! Personally I'm much too distressed.'

Under any other circumstances his look of dismay would have been almost comic, but for the moment Natalie's sense of humour lay dormant.

'Your capacity for wine doesn't seem similarly affected.' Edward was acid, disappointment and hunger giving a marked feline tone to his well-bred voice.

'It helps mitigate the blow of being regarded as a "loose end".' Natalie fingered the modest solitaire diamond on her left hand rather ostentatiously. 'Do go on, tell me all.'

A little of Edward's usual polish seemed to tarnish, and he ran a finger round under his now slightly limp collar.

'There's really not much more to say, except that I

shall be working closely in conjunction with Lisa's father in the new job, which makes it all rather a convenient arrangement.'

'What does he do?' asked Natalie with interest.

'He's G. K. Beaumont, actually, the Managing Director.' Edward's eyes slid away from hers and he shifted a little in his seat.

'Ah!' The single syllable held a world of amused comprehension and put Edward immediately on the defensive.

'It's not at all like that, Natalie. It's not in any way a case of nepotism, merely that I happen to be exactly the type of person required for this particular opening, and I was in the right place at the right time.'

'And you just happened to catch the fancy of the Managing Director's daughter. Really, Edward, your passion for the neat and tidy has surpassed itself this time. There's just Natalie, the loose end, to cast off and everything is ship-shape and Bristol fashion. Congratulations—on all counts.'

She took off her engagement ring and handed it to him.

To her fascination Edward flushed a dull red, and for once was at a loss for words.

'It was my intention to ask you to—er—keep the ring, my dear. I would like you to very much.'

'What as?' enquired Natalie pleasantly, draining her glass, 'a constant reminder that I was rejected in favour of a newer, smaller and infinitely more eligible model? You can be quite remarkably insensitive on occasion!'

'Please, Natalie.' Edward's eyes were aggrieved. 'I've been hoping we could conduct this obviously painful business without acrimony, in as civilised a manner as possible——'

'I bet you were!' she interrupted, eyes kindling.

'Please let's not descend to childish insult.'

'Give me one good reason why not! I don't, at this particular moment, feel the least bit sensible and well balanced, nor can I see why I should be in the least civilised, dear Edward. I'm bored to my toenails with being civilised!'

Natalie's rising wrath was fuelled by the transient courage of several glasses of unaccustomed wine on an empty stomach, and she took a deep breath as she launched into a further tirade. 'You may keep your modest little piece of jewellery—perhaps you'll be able to put it towards the cost of the one you've bought for little Lisa. Or is Daddy paying for that?'

'Now look here——' began Edward hotly, rising precipitately to his feet.

'No, Edward, you look here!' Natalie rose with him, the last remnants of her control magnificently departed. Colour was running high along her cheekbones and her eyes glittered as she glared at him, eye to eye across the small table. 'You've had three years of my life, more or less, while I've tried to modify my tastes to suit yours. I've bought discreet, well-cut, boring clothes you consider suitable, eaten all the gussied-up food you like, gone to concerts of chamber music I detest, and I've even tried to like the people you consider worth knowing—and heaven knows that was a struggle sometimes! Not once, in all the time I've known you, have you tried to change one of your preferences to suit mine. This is the age of the liberated woman I'm told, and I begin to think I've spent far too long chained to a male chauvinist pig of the first water. In short, Mr Herrick,' her husky voice became noticeably scratchy as it rose in volume, 'take your diamond, such as it is, and your executive suitcase and your air of well-bred distaste and go away—back to your Lolita, and the camels, and . . . and. . . .'

At this point Natalie's flow of invective dissolved into unaccustomed, regrettably noisy tears and she subsided into her chair, head on the table, sobbing into the scarlet table napkin with all the uninhibited violence of an overdose of alcohol.

Mute with horror, Edward stood rooted to the spot, an appalled look on his clear-cut features. Suddenly he came to life, and to the accompaniment of Natalie's fury of weeping he hurriedly put on his jacket, picked up his suitcase, then looked irresolutely for a moment at the diamond ring lying on the table near the dishevelled dark red head. He hesitated a moment longer, then his face hardened and he put the ring in his pocket.

'Goodbye, Natalie.' He regarded her downbent head with cold disapproval, and receiving no response beyond a slight rise in the decibel rate of her distress, he shrugged and let himself quietly out of the flat.

Gradually Natalie's sobs began to diminish, eventually dying away to a spasmodic hiccup, and she just sat, shattered, like the survivor of some violent holocaust. After a long, numb interval she straightened and, chin propped on her hands, stared round the room from beneath heavily swollen eyelids with the air of someone seeing it for the first time. It was furnished with a curious mixture of Maggie's flamboyance and her own slightly less assertive taste, and normally Natalie loved it. Tonight it was a prison made garish by the bright evening sunshine, itself almost an affront to the feeling of chill desolation that lay on her spirit like a pall.

Natalie cleared the table wearily and washed the dishes, automatically putting the diminutive kitchen to rights. She stripped off the silk dress, screwed it up in a bundle and hurled it into the corner of the bedroom she shared with Maggie, then stood under the shower in the cramped little bathroom, trying to sluice away the overwhelming feeling of loss in the cascade of cool water. When she emerged she was surprised to find it was still relatively early. A whole lifetime seemed to have passed since the morning. Aimlessly Natalie wandered barefoot into the living room dressed in a short Swiss cotton housecoat, her hair piled up in a precarious knot on top of her head, and stood for a moment, undecided. It dawned on her that some of the pangs she was feeling might possibly be hunger, so she went back to the kitchen to make herself a sandwich. In the act of filling the kettle she stopped abruptly. To blazes with tea, she thought fiercely. There was most of a bottle of Burgundy asking to be consumed, so she might as well consume it.

Natalie carried her little feast back to the other room

and put *Traviata* on the record player, the mellow wine
and the passionate beauty of the voices of Domingo
and Cotrubas enacting the doomed love story all
combining to soothe her raw hurt to a stage where it
was relatively bearable.

'*Piangi, piangi!*' sang Germont Père to Violetta.

How sensible, thought Natalie hazily. When one is
unhappy the Italians say 'cry, cry' instead of 'hush,
don't cry', like the self-controlled British. Not that I
needed any Italian urging me to cry tonight, she
thought wryly. I made rather a superb job of it all by
myself. Funny, I can't ever remember crying like that
before in my entire life. Well, perhaps once. Her face
grew pensive, then cleared as she chased an unwanted
memory by means of another glass of wine.

Perhaps this is how people become alcoholics, she
mused, after the opera had finished. To her dismay the
wine had run out too. However, her mood had
improved to the stage where it was possible to consider
what she should do next. The first inescapable hurdle
was the fortnight's holiday looming in front of her to
get through alone.

Natalie sat contemplating the alternatives. One was
to postpone the holiday and return to work. This was
instantly rejected, as even the remotest possibility of
meeting Edward was something to be avoided. Her
sister Cordelia lived in Paris; she could always go there,
she mused. Finally, with the slight, inexplicable
reluctance the prospect invariably induced, she came to
the decision that, deep down, she had known from the
beginning was the only one possible. Tomorrow she
would go home to Arden-under-Hill in the Cotswolds
and spend the time with her mother, something she had
done very little since Edward's advent, in fact, not since
she had left home to go to college some seven years
before. Natalie felt guilty as she thought of her mother.

Her father had been a doctor who had died tragically
young in a car accident, leaving Mrs Ross to carry on
her life with her two small daughters as best she could.
Compensation had been paid by the firm owning the
lorry which had ended her husband's life, and Julia

Ross had been able to continue living in the village she had first known as a bride, eking out her means by writing and illustrating children's books. She also threw herself into community life, and now her daughters were no longer at home she was involved in every committee and organisation that a twenty-four-hour day allowed.

Natalie decided it was too late to ring her mother that night; Julia regarded anything after ten as an emergency. The morning would be soon enough, and in the meantime she would escape to bed before Maggie came home. Explanations were the last thing she felt like coping with tonight, and at the moment her one desire in life was the mercy of sleep.

The following morning Maggie was quietly up and away to her hospital ward while Natalie was pretending to be still asleep. When she finally persuaded herself to get out of bed, she winced and clutched her head, feeling decidedly the worse for wear. Her pallid face and pink swollen eyes were examined in the mirror with dismay, and after effecting what repairs were possible, while consuming several cups of tea, with some aspirin to soothe her thumping head, she rang her mother. Three calls in the space of half an hour drew a blank. Natalie was unsurprised. Her mother led a very busy life, and she could be anywhere in the village, involved in heaven knew what activity. Swiftly packing her new clothes, and leaving an explanatory note for Maggie, Natalie left the flat tidy and went down to the car.

It was well after midday before she finally left London and was on her way to the Cotswolds. She was wearing a new dress, an olive-green sheer cotton lawn that floated, bias-cut, from a V-shaped crocheted yoke. The sash that came with it was tied, Apache style, round her forehead, leaving her hair to stream unconfined down her back. Enormous dark glasses completed the outfit, and she smiled at the fleeting glimpse of herself in the driving mirror as she turned on to the M4 and headed in the direction of Oxford. Edward would have difficulty in recognising her. Always supposing he was likely to want the opportunity.

CHAPTER TWO

THE June day was clear and sunny and she drove competently and swiftly, soon reaching Oxford and taking the road towards Stratford-upon-Avon. There had been no answer from her mother's telephone, but Natalie was philosophic about her busy parent's whereabouts; someone in the village would know where she was to be found. Branching off the main road some ten miles short of Stratford, she wound her way along meandering country roads full of dog-roses and meadowsweet. High summer was green and gold all around her as she drove more slowly now, her initial reluctance dispersing and enjoyment taking its place, together with relief as some of the tension of the last twenty-four hours began to drain away, leaving her a little tired, but not as achingly unhappy as she had expected.

Natalie drove through the busy little village of Arden-under-Hill, her eyes alert for her mother's small figure, but with no success. Outside the village she changed gear to cope with the suddenly steep hill that gave it its name and climbed steadily up past Arden House, set well back from the road in its beautiful gardens, until she came to her goal, Hill Cottage, perched at the exact summit. She turned thankfully into the drive, relieved to see that her mother's car was there already, and parked neatly behind it, stretching as she got out. She pulled the gauzy material of her dress away from her warm body, then stiffened. From the back of the lath-and-plaster cottage came the sound of voices and music. Oh no! Natalie thought wildly. For pity's sake don't let it be the Garden Club's annual tea, or a W.I. committee meeting, or something.

Leaving her belongings in the car, she crept silently round the side of the house, stopping suddenly in astonishment. The entire garden seemed to be filled with large canvases painted with trees and greenery. They leaned against apple-trees, the fence, against garden furniture, even the lawnmower. The lawn itself was covered with newspaper and buckets of paint. Her mother and a tall, muscular man were dipping industriously into these and creating yet more greenery on two canvases propped in front of them. The music— Mendelssohn, noted Natalie automatically—was issuing from a transistor on the path, and both artists were so absorbed in their labours they were unaware of the onlooker. Julia Ross was attired in old tennis shoes, paint-spattered jeans and an ancient collarless shirt, presumably her husband's, in lieu of a smock. The man alongside her, whistling tunelessly in counterpoint to the radio, was similarly dressed as to jeans and track shoes, but his magnificent back and shoulders gleamed brown and bare in the afternoon sun, muscles rippling as he rhythmically bent to load his brush, sweeping paint on to canvas with more panache than artistry.

Natalie froze. It was a considerable time since she had last seen him, but there was no mistaking the grace of the athletic figure, without even seeing his face. He was all too heart-stoppingly familiar, and she groaned inwardly, casting an eye skywards in reproach. Someone up there was really piling it on! The half-clothed figure struck an immediate chord in her memory, giving instant recall of something she had spent some time trying to forget. By the slow smile spreading over the tanned face as he turned, arrested, brush in mid-air as he caught sight of her, Natalie had little hope that he had forgotten either. She coughed, ignoring him. Her mother spun round, her small, expressive face instantly alight with such radiant welcome that Natalie's throat closed and tears threatened as Julia Ross threw her brush into a jar of spirit and flew towards her tall daughter, arms open wide.

'Darling, darling, what a lovely surprise—I'll have to keep my hands away from you, they're covered with paint, and you look so gorgeous. Let me kiss you— bend down!'

Natalie bent obediently, hugging her mother, glad of her large tinted spectacles that obscured her eyes and partially hid her face from Julia as the latter stood back and inspected her daughter with pleasure.

'I rang several times, Mother, but no reply, so I just came,' said Natalie simply.

'Of course you did!' Julia looked behind Natalie expectantly. 'Is Edward with you—he arrived safely I presume?'

'No—I mean yes, he arrived safely, but no, he's not with me.' Natalie stopped short as her mother's dark eyes, identical to her own, narrowed questioningly.

'Too busy, no doubt,' said Julia quickly, then belatedly remembered her painting companion.

'Forgive me, Nick,' she smiled delightedly at the tall man who stood silently watching, 'I had no idea Natalie was coming; I don't see nearly as much of her as I'd like, so please forgive me. Of course, you both remember each other, I've no doubt.'

'No doubt at all. Hello, young Nat.' The man moved forward, smiling in a way Natalie remembered only too well, the sun glinting behind him on ash-fair hair, his eyes half-closed as though he were trying to see behind her dark lenses.

'Nicholas Marlowe, no less,' said Natalie, holding out her hand. 'It must be all of—oh, I can't remember how many years since you stopped coming to Arden House. How are you?'

She felt quite proud of her sangfroid considering the various emotions rigorously repressed inside her.

He just stood there, looking at her, still smiling faintly, regretfully refusing the long slender hand offered to him.

'Like your mother, I can't shake hands. I'll defer that pleasure until I'm a little less encrusted with paint. You've grown up, Natalie.'

'People do, in time,' she said lightly. 'Now tell me what on earth you two are doing?'

Julia had been looking from one to the other with bright-eyed interest, now she motioned Natalie to a closer inspection of the still-wet canvases.

'Well, darling, what do you think?'

Natalie examined each one with grave attention.

'I'm not sure just exactly what I'm supposed to say,' she said slowly, her eyes dancing, 'rather more Rolf Harris than Constable or Turner, I feel. But why all the same subject?'

'A wood near Athens, of course!' Nick's deep voice came from rather too close behind her and Natalie had to force herself not to move instinctively away. She laughed and gave a theatrical groan of comprehension.

'Of course! That was Mendelssohn's *Midsummer Night's Dream* on the radio. Don't tell me you're involved in theatricals again, Mother, especially Shakespeare!'

'Why not?' Julia bridled defensively. 'This is Shakespeare country, after all, and everyone loves the *Dream*—however, before I get on my hobbyhorse let's go in and get cleaned up, then I'll give you some tea, or a drink, as you fancy.'

'I'm not really respectable enough, Mrs Ross. . . .' Nicholas began, after a fleeting look at Natalie's withdrawn expression, but his hesitation was swept aside.

'Nonsense! Just wash and put your shirt on and you'll be quite respectable enough for us, won't he, Natalie?'

'Of course.' Natalie smiled woodenly and allowed herself to be swept into the kitchen, where she volunteered to make the tea while her mother went upstairs to change, and Nick Marlowe washed in the downstairs cloakroom.

Natalie filled the kettle and put out cups abstractedly, silently cursing whatever fates had sent their guest across her path again, and this day of all days. All these tests of my moral fibre must be very character-building, she thought, so immersed in her sombre thoughts that she jumped, her nerve ends raw and quivering as the object of them reappeared unnoticed and stood smiling at her sardonically as he lounged against the counter-top. There was an awkward little silence while they eyed each other warily.

'I'm still unforgiven?' His eyes were unwavering and intent as she turned away and busied herself, arranging biscuits on a plate with exquisite care.

'Of course not.' Natalie kept her attention on her unnecessary task. 'I just find myself unexpectedly embarrassed, considering it was all in the dim and distant past.'

'Unnecessary. Look at me.'

He moved closer and turned her unwilling face up to his. Natalie gasped involuntarily. In the garden his slightly over-long hair had flopped over his forehead, but now it had been damped and combed away a long, jagged red weal was revealed over one eye. It extended down over the bridge of his nose, and stitch marks were still evident along its length.

'What happened, Nick?'

'Would you believe a car accident?' He smiled humourlessly, then suddenly whipped the sunglasses away from her face.

Natalie reached for them frantically.

'Please! Let me put them back on—my face is not open to the public at the moment.'

Very deliberately Nick replaced the huge glasses on the short, straight nose, a lingering finger idly tracing the sprinkling of freckles, then he subsided into a kitchen chair stiffly with a gesture of apology, his eyes hooded.

'Forgive me. I've been standing around a bit too long today. Now then, Natalie, to echo your question, what happened?' He studied her averted face, picking up her ringless left hand. 'Your mother told me you were engaged. Presumably there's a connection?'

'Yes,' said Natalie flatly. 'Right up until yesterday I was engaged. Today I'm not. . . .' She broke off with relief as her mother came in wearing a trim sleeveless cotton shirt and skirt, her grey-sprinkled red curls neatly brushed.

'Pour out, there's a love,' she instructed briskly. 'Now how long can you stay, darling?'

'About a fortnight, if that's all right.'

'It's not only all right, it's a godsend right now, when

I can do with all the help I can get. The Dramatic Society is putting some scenes from *A Midsummer Night's Dream* on on the twenty-first in aid of the church restoration fund. The vicar was quite desperate, as apparently the tower will emulate the one in Pisa if something isn't done soon. Nick has kindly given us permission to give the performance in the grounds of Arden House, so let's all pray the weather holds up. If it's wet we fall back on the Village Hall.'

Natalie turned to Nick in surprise, constraint forgotten.

'How come it's your permission—what about your uncle, old Mr Marlowe? I rather thought he'd told you never to darken his door again some years ago.'

'You are out of touch! My uncle died earlier this year, and to everyone's surprise, notably mine, left everything to me, comprising of the house and quite a respectable competence to go with it. Apparently I was the only one of the possible legatees who didn't smarm round him, according to the will. Also, in his words, I'd given up that confounded foolishness by then, not to mention the inestimable advantage of being his only surviving relative with the name Marlowe. So here I am, in residence.'

'You *live* here?' Natalie made no effort to conceal her dismay, convinced by now that fate was indeed bent on playing jokes on her with a vengeance.

'I do indeed; nothing like rural seclusion, I find, both for relaxation and mental stimulation. You should try it some time.' He lounged back in his chair, patently enjoying her discomfiture, a hatefully smug smile tugging at the corners of his mouth.

'It will be very good for Nick to recuperate here,' said Julia, frowning in surprise at her daughter's lack of manners. 'More tea, anyone?'

The other two declined, and Natalie helped wash up while Julia regaled her with more details of the forthcoming production.

'Nicholas has been a tremendous help. He's condensed the scenes I needed into a workable playlet, as I didn't think we had the resources for the whole thing.

We've concentrated on the scenes in the wood only, and jettisoned the court bits.'

'What do you do with yourself these days, then, Nick? Are you just playing at Lord of the Manor?' Natalie was curious.

Nick rose to his feet and stood, looking at the lovely cool picture the girl made as she sat on a corner of the pine table, one foot in its gilt sandal idly swinging back and forth, her face a blank mask of polite attention.

'I retired from the track a couple of years ago, Natalie,' he said, an oddly defensive note in his voice. 'I write novels now—two kinds, to be precise.'

Natalie smiled mockingly, her voice spiced with a faint but definite malice.

'Congratulations. I thought that nothing or no one would ever have managed to separate you from your aim in life. Formula One World Championship or nothing, wasn't it, if I remember correctly—I was quite surprised when I read somewhere that you'd packed it all in.'

He shrugged indifferently as Julia listened with interest, obviously keenly aware of the slight undercurrent lying beneath the conversation.

'I didn't realise you knew each other so well. When Nick used to spend his holidays here Cordelia was the one nearer to him in age.'

'Oh, I made myself a complete nuisance to Nick, didn't I?' appealed Natalie carelessly. 'At seventeen I convinced myself that the glamorous Nicholas Marlowe was the only man in the world for me. What an irritating little bore I must have been!'

'Never that, Natalie.' Nick's tanned face was unreadable as he looked steadily at her, then he glanced at the kitchen clock and whistled. 'It's late! Mrs Corby likes me to be ready for my meal at seven on the dot on the evenings she cooks for me. I must get rid of the paint before eating, so I'd better be on my way.'

Julia rose to see him out.

'I sincerely hope I haven't tired you out doing our Picasso bit, but really no one else in the village seems the least bit artistic,' apologised Julia.

'Of course not, it's great; gets rid of all one's inhibitions, sloshing paint around with abandon. You can co-opt Natalie into the team tomorrow.' Nick bent to kiss Julia's cheek. 'Goodnight, Mrs R., I'll leave you in peace with your prodigal. Goodnight, Natalie. Will you allow me to say, with utmost sincerity, that the little girl has grown into a very beautiful lady?'

'How kind. Thank you, and goodnight.' Natalie's colour rose a little, but her voice was composed, even aloof.

Both women watched the tall man walk slowly through the garden in the direction of the gate in the hedge that connected Hill Cottage with Arden House, then Julia Ross turned to her daughter in long-suppressed enquiry.

'Now then, my love. Suppose you take off those very effective glasses and tell me what's happened and how I can help put it right.'

Natalie did as she was bid, smiling ruefully at the expression on her mother's face. Julia made no immediate comment, but went immediately into the dining-room and reappeared with a bottle of brandy.

'I keep it for emergency,' she said, 'and this looks as though it might be something like that. You look shattered, Natalie. Get some ice out of the fridge, love, and some ginger ale, and we'll have a nice long drink in the garden while you tell me as much as you want to tell me.'

Natalie put her arm round her mother and hugged her.

'Maggie insists that confession does the appearance good as well as the soul, and both my face and my self-esteem need a little restoration. Let's hope catharsis is the answer.'

They did a little quick scene-shifting in the garden to liberate two garden chairs and sat with faces turned towards the evening sun.

'In short, Edward's jilted me,' Natalie began without preamble.

Julia gazed at her daughter in affronted disbelief and took a long drink of her brandy mixture.

'How dare he! Not that I'm sorry. He isn't good enough for you; a sexless, opinionated tailor's dummy, I've always thought.'

'Mother!' Natalie was astonished by her parent's vehemence.

'I'm sorry, but even though I've done my best to like him I just couldn't manage it. And what possible reason did he give for breaking the engagement, Natalie?' Julia was literally quivering with indignation.

'He met a girl in Qatar, small, nubile, twenty years old, incredibly pretty, and by the look on his face when he described her, a sexpot. To crown all, her father is managing director out in Doha and has given E. Herrick, Esq., a marvellous new job working under him.' Natalie gave a mirthless little laugh. 'How in the world could I expect to compete with such a list of advantages? Mother, you must admit I was defeated, horse, foot and guns.'

There was a desolate little catch in the husky voice which made Julia Ross look searchingly at the long, graceful figure lounging wearily in the chair, dark eyes heavy in her creamy face, her freckles standing out sharply as they always did in times of stress.

'Are you desperately unhappy, Natalie?' she asked with deep concern. 'You've given up quite a large slice of your life to Edward. Of course, it's utterly characteristic of him to throw that aside with complete disregard for anything but his own desires. However, if this child had been less well connected he'd probably have had a torrid little affair and come home to you to resume as though nothing had happened.'

Natalie finished her drink while she digested her mother's comments.

'I can hardly pretend to be on top of the world. A small consolation is the way I subjected him to the most uninhibited scene, throwing back his ring and coming out with a string of home truths in a very vulgar manner. He was absolutely disgusted and couldn't make his getaway fast enough. I'd drunk a large quantity of wine and it transformed me into a raging termagant, then I woke up with a ghastly hangover this morning. These eyelids are the result of headache as well as the crying jag. Frankly, I think it was my pride that took the hardest knock, possibly, but it's difficult to wave three years of my life away without a backward glance.'

Julia nodded in understanding.

'Of course it is, darling, but in time I'm sure you'll be glad. Except that I hate to see you hurt, I myself can't help feeling relieved. I found it impossible to take to the man.'

'You never said so, Mother.' Natalie was curious. 'Why not?'

'I knew he just wasn't the right man to make you happy, but he was your choice and it's your life. But perhaps now you can live it the way you want to for a change; start being my Natalie again, not the prim and proper creature you turned into to please that man. Has he ever tried to get you into bed?'

Natalie turned scarlet, then began to laugh hysterically.

'Mother, Mother, really, is that the sort of thing to say to your daughter? To keep the record straight—no, he hasn't. It was all to be deferred to the proper time.'

'Whenever that would have been!' Julia snorted as she rose to her feet. 'Let's go and get some food together and expunge Edward Herrick from the records. Myself, I'm delighted. In the fullness of time you will be too, my love.'

'I hope you're right,' said Natalie doubtfully, then changed the subject. 'Now tell me why Nick Marlowe and you are so thick. What's he doing here, anyway?'

They went in to the house and began preparing a light meal of cheese and salad.

'The poor lad's had a harrowing time—I'll tell you in a moment,' began Julia, swiftly washing lettuce while Natalie laid the table, 'but first I have some lovely news for you. Cordelia is expecting a baby in January!'

Natalie gave a whoop of joy, instantly forgetting her melancholy.

'That's marvellous! She and Jean-Luc must be over

the moon. I was aware they'd been longing for a child for ages—is she all right?'

'They rang up from Paris last night. Apparently they wanted to wait until it was completely certain before announcing the glad news.'

They sat down to their meal, happily discussing the forthcoming event. Cordelia was married to Jean-Luc Cassel, a French businessman, and their home was in Paris. A case of love at first sight for them both, the only cloud on their horizon had been Cordelia's failure to become pregnant after two years of marriage.

Natalie made coffee, while her mother produced a raspberry tart and insisted she eat a generous slice after such a light supper.

'It's from the crop I froze last year; wasn't it fortunate I made a pie yesterday? I made two, in fact, and gave one to Nicholas.'

'Ah yes. Nicholas,' said Natalie purposefully. 'It was something of a blow when I came creeping home for sanctuary and found him, of all people, in possession. Yet another male who rejected me. Very bad for my ego to be surrounded by men who consider me unsuitable wife material.'

Julia stared at Natalie nonplussed.

'But you were only a child when he was here before!'

'I was seventeen, Mother, more than old enough to dream of him all day long. I was obsessed with him, thought he was God's gift to womankind. To be fair, he was very good-natured, used to play tennis with me and let me trail everywhere after him, as he was a good deal older, at least eight years or so, not to mention the fact that he was the up-and-coming name in the world of Formula One motor racing. I was besotted, to say the least, and when he was walking me home one night, there was a moon and he kissed me goodnight and I completely lost my wits. I took one kiss to be a wholesale declaration of love and threw myself into his arms declaring my undying devotion and eager willingness to forget all about going to college to spend my life as a sort of camp-follower of the racing circuits, only as his bride, of course.'

'Good heavens,' said Julia, awed, 'what on earth did he do?'

'Not a lot. He laughed.'

'Oh!'

'Yes, oh! My tender feelings were badly lacerated as he kindly explained that he was a bit old for me, I was just a little young to be anyone's wife, that one day I'd meet someone nearer my own age, etc., etc., and in the meantime I should carry on with my plans for my career. I thought my heart was broken and my life ruined, silly little idiot.'

'Oh, darling, and I never knew a thing!' Julia was flabbergasted. 'I must have been going round with my eyes shut. But surely you're not still put out with him, love, it was all a very long time ago, and he obviously tried to let you down as lightly as possible.'

'No, of course not. It just seemed like the last straw to come home to lick my wounds after being cast casually aside like an old shoe, and there in the garden, very much at home, is yet another man who once gave me the heave-ho too. You must admit it didn't exactly pour balm on my wounds. My ego is at rock bottom!'

Natalie looked across at her mother and smiled with genuine amusement for the first time in twenty-four hours.

'There must be someone who would fancy a tall, well-built redhead, Mother, surely!'

'Personally, I got the impression Nick wasn't exactly repelled this afternoon,' said Julia, eyes twinkling, 'unless of course, you find his scar a bit off-putting. I think he's inclined to be a bit over-conscious about it.'

'It doesn't affect me one way or another.' Natalie stood up to stretch and yawn. 'Besides, it has something of the effect of a duelling scar, like a romantic Regency hero, probably very attractive to most women. For myself I'm off the opposite sex. I'll give all of them a wide berth for the time being, at least until I've built up my fragile self-confidence. Now, do you think I could have a bath, and then I think I'll go to bed. Sleep was a bit elusive last night, and I'm beginning to feel like a rag doll.'

While Natalie's father had been alive the family lived right in the village in a large house, half of which had been given over to the consulting rooms and surgery of the practice Dr Ross had run with the aid of a young, newly-qualified assistant. After the tragic accident Julia had needed somewhere small and reasonably priced for herself and the two little girls, but was reluctant to leave the area where she had been so happy. Old Mr Marlowe, of Arden House, with quite uncharacteristic benevolence, had let her have Hill Cottage at a peppercorn rent, and gratefully she had settled there to make a new life for herself and the children. Natalie had only the haziest memories of her father, scrubbed hard hands that tickled and comforted her, and a laughing voice, were all she actually remembered, though there were photographs in plenty, and a very sensitive pencil sketch executed by Julia on one of the rare occasions when Dr Ross had been permitted to sit in the garden unmolested by the telephone.

The small cottage was in a good state of preservation and Natalie loved it intensely. The front door opened straight into the sitting room, which was small and cosy, its size diminished by a large cowled stone fireplace and by the low black beams in the ceiling with the original hooks where sides of bacon had once hung. At one time the home of some of the servants attached to the big house, great efforts had been made to keep the original atmosphere. The adjoining small dining-room had a glass panel let into the wall to show the original construction, but a very modern swing door led into the kitchen, which had been enlarged by the addition of a glass-roofed extension with one wall consisting entirely of windows that seemed to bring the lovely old-fashioned garden right into the room.

As Natalie carried her suitcase up the narrow steep stairs that led directly out of the living room, the scent of dew-heavy roses filled the house and lingered on the air. There were two bedrooms upstairs and a bathroom had been made by sacrificing a large-airing-cupboard. Julia's bedroom was small and compact with a double bed and fitted cupboards to utilise the space under the eaves. The other room was longer than its width and ran along the back of the house, the sprigged curtains at its two small windows moving gently in the evening breeze. A skirted dressing-table divided the two beds, and apart from one small wardrobe practically all the wall-space was taken up with bookshelves that held all the books Natalie and Cordelia had read from babyhood on, from Beatrix Potter to Graham Greene.

Natalie gave a great sigh as she entered the familiar room, unchanged in every detail right down to the small china pig that had held her first pocket-money. Julia came behind her, looking at her daughter closely.

'I hope you'll sleep well, darling. Don't worry if you want to get up and make a drink, or anything—you won't disturb me. And even if you do it doesn't matter. Now let me help you hang up your things.'

Natalie opened her case and took out brand-new unfamiliar garments, most of them with their price-tags still attached.

'I had a little shopping spree,' she said apologetically in answer to her mother's look of enquiry as she held up a cinnamon velour jump-suit. 'Two sprees, really. I bought a lot of new things for my holiday with Edward—my usual stuff, more geared to theatre-going and little lunches in fashionable places than a couple of weeks lazing at home with Mum.' She gave Julia a little squeeze. 'What do you think of this lot? What you might call my post-Edward gear, as I took the first lot back to the shop and swapped it all for these things this morning before I left town.'

Julia looked at the array with approval.

'It's about time you started dressing like a normal girl occasionally. They all look gorgeous. Those two dresses are really stunning—very unusual with your hair.'

She held up a dress in Mexican semi-diaphanous cotton that hung in a myriad of tiny fluid pleats to its whirling satin-bound hem. The colour was the exact shade of a parma violet, the ribbons a shade or two lighter.

'Very clever, darling.' Julia held it up against her tall daughter. 'The other one, in that heavenly coral shade—is that exactly the same?'

'I'm afraid so.' Natalie smiled sheepishly. 'The sales lady was an old hand. She brought it out 'just in case I preferred the colour'. Of course I was too spineless to resist either. Goodness knows where I'll wear them, but I rather felt entitled to a wild moment. They weren't exactly cheap!'

'That's patently obvious,' Julia chuckled, and kissed Natalie's cheek. 'Now go straight to sleep after your bath, darling, and I'll cook you a proper breakfast in the morning before I get to grips with the Arden Players in W. Shakespeare's *Dream*.'

Natalie pulled a face, gathering up her toilet things to depart bath-wards.

'I suppose this room hasn't been slept in since Cordelia and Jean-Luc were here?'

Julia's eyes sparkled naughtily.

'They didn't sleep here then, either. I did. Jean-Luc refuses to sleep apart from Cordelia, and thinks twin beds are the basic cause of marital discord. He was extremely Gallic and explicit about it—not that Cordelia minded, she seemed to be in total agreement. So we swapped.'

'You'd think they'd be over that stage by now!' Natalie felt absurdly embarrassed, much to her mother's amusement.

'Some people never get over that "stage", as you put it, Natalie. A good marriage has a successful physical side to it always, in varying degrees.'

'Yes, Mother.' Natalie's face was mocking as she went into the bathroom. 'I can only conclude that these earthly little pronouncements in your conversation are a direct result of your lifelong passion for Shakespeare!'

CHAPTER THREE

LYING in her childhood bed, Natalie lay awake far into the night, obsessed by memories long shut away in the far recesses of her mind. If a new pain were really the best means of assuaging an old one, she thought restlessly, meeting Nick Marlowe had certain fringe benefits, if only as a diversion from the thought of Edward and his sudden defection. For years the glamorous, dangerous advance of Nick's progress on the Grand Prix circuit had been only too easy to chart. The media were full of accounts of him, television cameras zooming in on the wide white grin beneath the wild blond hair, eyes gleaming in victory triumph, a laurel wreath round his neck as he shook a bottle of champagne in time-honoured, wasteful way over everyone in sight. Natalie had watched that little scene a couple of times on television, noting with distaste the blonde or brunette inevitably on hand to drape herself over him as the cameras clicked. At one time a visit to the hairdresser or the dentist inevitably yielded up a glossy magazine with an article on Nick Marlowe, the most eligible, jetsetting bachelor of the racing fraternity, his name coupled with countless beautiful creatures, but never to one particular one for long.

Natalie flopped moodily over on to her stomach, her mind refusing to shut off and let her sleep. She remembered vividly the furore of two years before that greeted the news of Nick's retirement from the track at the peak of his career. It was typical that he gave no explanation, smiling into the camera with the well-known grin that somehow failed to reach his eyes, eluding the reporters' questions adroitly, merely saying it was time to quit while he was ahead. She relived the violent relief that had filled her as she heard the deep, laconic voice, and the eyes that seemed to look straight at her only from the television set, before Edward switched it over to BBC 2 and a concert of Elizabethan madrigals. Since then Nick had disappeared from the public eye until today, as far as she was concerned. She was unsurprised to find he had taken to writing books; hardly too unexpected from someone who'd read English at university. She wondered idly what the books were like, then got out of bed and wandered over to the window to lean out, looking at the stars, and breathing in the scent of midsummer.

The evocative scent of dew-damp grass brought back another night, years before, when a younger, bemused Natalie had walked blissfully through the Arden House gardens with Nick and lingered at the garden gate to the cottage, all her young being focussed on the life he was describing, of how he was just beginning to make his presence felt in the competitive jungle of the racing world. He had been staying with his uncle for a short rest from the hectic programme of races, and had naturally gravitated towards the two girls at Hill Cottage for company. Cordelia had begun to work as receptionist to the doctors in the village, so it was Natalie, newly released from school, her A-levels behind her, who was available to walk and play tennis and croquet, accompany him on leisurely drives round the countryside, to her delirious delight. She had gradually grown to realise that Nick was becoming more and more aware of her as a woman, if only a young, unfledged one, rather than the tomboy he'd watched grow up over the years. Odd little silences occurred when their eyes met, hands touched more often than before, and though she vaguely sensed the restraint he exerted on himself, she knew Nick no longer saw her as a little girl.

One evening they had been playing tennis on the old grass court in the gardens, a welcome relief to Nick from the acrimony shown to him that day by his uncle at his refusal to give up racing and turn his energies to something more conventional and respectable.

'The old devil wants me to conform, Nat,' he explained, an arm casually round her shoulders, unaware of the almost sickening excitement he was inducing in her by the mere nearness of his warm, hard body.

'You must be fair. Perhaps he's afraid you'll be injured, Nick.' How desperately Natalie had strived to sound judicious and adult, and as though she were completely accustomed to men touching her. Her wide, dark eyes had turned up to his in the half-light at the moment his head bent nearer to hear what she was saying. They were both suddenly silent, tense, as Nick stared down at her with his light eyes darkening, a strange expression dawning in them, making her tremble as both his arms locked round her and she was held fast against him.

'This is all wrong.' His voice was rough and husky. 'You're much too young——'

'Nearly eighteen.' She had brushed his remark aside, pressing herself even closer to him.

'It's still not old enough to be doing this—at least, not with me.' Harsh and admonitary as he tried to be, his arms had failed to slacken and his muscular, athlete's frame had vibrated in unison with hers, as though the same electric current flowed through them both.

'I want you, Nick—please kiss me!' Someone else had taken Natalie over and was saying unheard-of things in her voice.

'You don't know what you're saying! You've always thought of me as a brother, Natalie.'

'Not since I was twelve years old, I haven't.' The other person in control of Natalie began to undulate her hips. Long legs, bare except for the briefest of tennis shorts, trembled against the muscled length of his, bare like her own, his only garments tennis shorts and singlet.

'No! Stop—you don't realise . . .' His disjointed gasps were anguished, and to her despair she felt him move away from her, then triumph flooded her as his hand had taken hers and drawn her away from the path, leading her deep into the shadows behind the box hedges, below the concealing branches of an ancient elm. Pulling her down on the grass alongside him, he'd taken her into his arms and kissed her, the first adult kiss of her entire life. Utterly amazed by the unguessed-at feelings streaking along all her nerves like flashes of lightning, her response was instinctive, her mouth opening to his, tentatively at first, then heatedly. Gasping in delight, she had wound herself even closer against him, her body curving into his as instinctively as though it knew where it belonged.

'Has anyone ever kissed you like this before?' His demand was curt and breathless, his hands moving up and down her back, hard and restless.

'No.'

'I shouldn't be either.' But he'd made no move to pull away. Her new sensations made Natalie bold, suddenly heady with the realisation of how she was affecting him; Nick, the up-and-coming celebrity, here in the hot, breathless dusk, his body urgent against hers.

'Don't talk. Just—just love me.' Her whisper burned in his ear, and suddenly she was flat on her back, his mouth fierce and demanding, while his hands searched and caressed and stroked her in places no one had ever touched before, her tennis shirt discarded and forgotten as his hands and mouth caressed her to frenzy. His body moved over on hers to her fierce satisfaction, but only for a fleeting moment or two before some semblance of sanity returned to him and he was on his feet in one graceful, violent movement, jerking her upright with him. The silence between them had been intense and taut as he dressed her again, buttoning her shirt with deliberation. Involuntarily his hands had run down her smooth thighs, sending tremors racing through them both, then wordlessly he took her back to Hill Cottage, an arm hard and possessive round her as he parted from her, still in silence, with only a last kiss for farewell.

For the following two days the pattern was set. During the day all possible time was spent together, playing tennis, walking, even gardening, then, in the same secluded spot, once the sun had gone down, and twilight lent them privacy, they retreated to the secret place under the elm, where Nick taught Natalie all the mysteries of physical pleasure a man and woman can give each other—all, that was, except the final one she craved, and which by some superhuman restraint Nick managed to withhold.

'Will I see you tomorrow?' Natalie had whispered on the third evening, confident of his answer in the flushed aftermath of his lovemaking that left both of them on edge and unfulfilled.

'No, little one. This is as far as it goes. Tomorrow I'm due at Silverstone and you must get back to your usual friends and forget all about this little episode.'

Natalie had lain, transfixed, her face agonised as she gazed at his sombre face, unable to take in what he was saying.

'Please, Nick, please take me with you,' she begged. 'I'd be no trouble. I'd follow you to the ends of the earth, you know that. I don't need to go to college, I'd make you a good wife, I promise you . . .'

His laugh had cut into her like a rapier thrust.

'Sweetheart, I'm very flattered, very touched, but it just wouldn't do. A baby like you on the merry-go-round I inhabit—you'd fall off only too quickly and get hurt. Go on to college, as you planned. Somewhere out there is a great guy waiting to be your Prince Charming, someone a whole lot more suitable than me. You'll thank me one day, believe me. This has been a magic little interlude, nothing more.'

Nick had refused to meet her eyes as numbly Natalie had picked herself up and tidied her clothes automatically. Looking at his blank, taut face unseeingly, she had bidden him a quiet, contained little goodbye and somehow or other made her way home blindly, to creep up to bed undetected to lick her wounds in private like a young maltreated animal, crying soundlessly far into the night. She had never seen Nick Marlowe in person again until today.

Natalie remained staring out into the dark night for some time, then pulled herself away from the window with an effort and returned to bed.

She woke early next morning, despite her difficulty in getting to sleep, forgetting how ear-splitting the dawn chorus could be as the birds welcomed the day in joyous chorale, the open windows letting the sound stream in to fill the bedroom. She lay quiet for a while, unwilling to disturb her mother, then could stay no longer and slid quietly out of bed, quickly wriggling into a pair of new pink cotton jeans and a pink and white gingham shirt. Carrying matching pink sneakers in her hand, she crept downstairs and winced as the ancient stair-treads creaked, tiptoeing into the kitchen which was flooded with light from the early morning sun.

Her careful stealth had been unnecessary, as her mother was already sitting at the pine table drinking tea from a Royal Worcester mug and reading the morning paper. She looked up in fond welcome at the sight of her pink-clad, barefoot daughter.

'You're early, Natalie. I hoped you'd have a lie-in. I tried not to wake you when I came down.'

'You didn't. It was those philharmonic birds!'

Natalie poured herself a mug of tea and sat down opposite her mother.

'Now what exactly are you going to be involved in today, Mother mine?'

'As it's Saturday there's a rehearsal this afternoon, at Arden House for the first time. That's why Nick and I were beavering away yesterday to finish the scenery.'

Natalie frowned.

'If you're doing the play in the garden, why on earth do you need painted scenery?'

'To use as flats, I think they call them. Just at the sides to mask the actors' entrances and give them cover. We did more than needed in case the weather drives us into the Village Hall.'

'Of course, stupid of me. Where exactly in the gardens are you staging it?'

'On the terrace above the old lawn tennis court. It's a natural platform and will be visible to everyone on the seats on the court, and Jack Cartwright from the radio shop is fixing up lights, also some microphones for audibility—we'll mask them with potted plants and shrubs, etc.'

Natalie gazed at her enterprising parent in awe.

'Did you think of all that by yourself?'

'No, not at all. I was originally going to stage it in the Village Hall, as usual, but Nick heard about it and came up with the suggestion of putting it on in the open air. And apparently we've been promised a long fine spell, to last at least another week, according to the weather men.'

'How long has Nick been living here?' asked Natalie casually.

'About two months. I'll get some breakfast.' Julia got up to busy herself at the cooker. 'He had this rather nasty accident and decided to come here to recuperate, as old Mr Marlowe left the house to him. Now he's doing it up a bit and thinks he'll live in it. Apparently his books bring him in enough to live on, and the inheritance was quite respectable.'

Natalie was consumed by intense curiosity, but had no intention of making it apparent.

'Who's going to be in the play?' she asked, deliberately changing the subject.

Julia put bacon to grill, and began beating eggs in a bright yellow bowl.

'I've rather departed from the norm, as I've made Oberon and Titania rustic characters, more or less in the same style as Bottom and his band of "workmen", then in contrast the lovers are played by two boys from King Edward's and two girls from the High School, all four of whom speak faultless English. Puck is played by a schoolboy, too—a lad with a very pointed face and a personality to match the part. He hardly needs to act.'

'Sounds highly entertaining,' said Natalie, looking with anticipation at the plate of crisp bacon and glossy scrambled egg Julia placed in front of her, 'of course, Nick has made it a sure-fire success by letting you put it on at Arden House. Everyone will flock there, if only to see what the grounds are like. Old Mr Marlowe had "No Trespassing" signs everywhere, so I don't suppose many people have ever been past the gate except the tradesmen.'

'Oh, the tickets have all been sold already,' said Julia.

'We did consider putting it on for two nights, but I think that might be pushing our luck too far with the weather.'

'You're probably right. Do I know any of the cast, by the way?'

'Oh yes—tea, love?—the Vicar is playing Bottom; remarkably well, too. Mr Hunscote from the General Store is Flute—that sort of age group for the mechanicals. The fairies are all played by village school-children, with great gusto. Then perhaps you remember Sam Wyatt from Lowfield Farm?'

Natalie thought for a moment while she buttered her toast.

'Wasn't I in school with him for a while when I was small? He was rather a weedy little boy with bright red hair, if I remember accurately.'

'That's the one.' Julia gave a little giggle. 'Except that he's six feet four now, the hair has toned down a bit, and he's the product of a smart agricultural college. Runs his father's farm like a machine. Sam doesn't really have very much of a local accent, but has to exaggerate it to match Melanie Dalton's. She's playing Titania.'

'Little Melanie from the White Lion? Good heavens, is she old enough?'

Julia poured more tea, smiling mischievously.

'For most things, I should think. She's quite a good little actress, but is rather too conscious of her physical charms. Tends to flaunt her—er—assets in the direction of the men a bit much. Come to rehearsal this afternoon—you may enjoy it.'

'Maybe.' Natalie was non-committal, unwilling to risk meeting Nicholas Marlowe again just yet. 'I thought I'd lie in the sun for a while and get a bit of warmth into my skin. I know I never tan, but I can usually manage a bit of a glow if I'm careful.'

Julia rose briskly, a neat small figure in a button-through leaf-green cotton dress.

'See how you feel. After a morning in the sun you may find you've had enough. Now I'd better see how my canvases have fared. They were dry last night, so I shouldn't think the dew will have affected our masterpieces—they were great fun to do.'

From the kitchen window Natalie watched her mother lovingly as she moved from canvas to canvas, inspecting each one carefully. It had been a surprise the night before to discover quite how strongly Julia had felt about Edward. It was a measure of her character that while she thought Natalie's happiness lay with him she had never given the least indication of her dislike. Admittedly Julia's relationship with Edward had been a little formal, unlike the teasing familiarity she enjoyed with Jean-Luc, but their meetings had not been frequent enough to make this obvious. Edward had a highly-developed aversion to the country and things rural, while Julia hardly ever went to London, so over the years, Natalie realised with surprise, they had met very seldom. One way and another Natalie began to feel she had been in the decided minority in her feelings towards Edward, as now she came to think of it, Cordelia had never seemed exactly rapturous towards him, and Jean-Luc was inclined to become excessively French in Edward's company.

'Let's hope his Lisa loves him,' thought Natalie, a sudden lump in her throat. She swallowed resolutely and went upstairs to search for a bikini now that the sun was high enough for her to lie out in the garden.

From the bedroom window she called to Julia.

'Do you want me to do anything about lunch?'

'Not really, I thought salad again—I'll bring some ham home with me, if that's all right with you. I'll take a chicken pie out of the freezer for tonight, and remind me to take out a joint of beef later for Sunday lunch tomorrow. The Vicar's coming.'

Natalie laughed as she stripped off her clothes. Julia was always inviting people to lunch, especially on Sundays; her excuse for having a joint, she usually explained. The Vicar was a single gentleman in his fifties, with a housekeeper who kept the Vicarage shining and spotless, but was not the most inspired of cooks.

After watching her diet assiduously for the past six

months, due to a comment from Edward that she was putting on weight, Natalie was gratified to find that the old bikini she finally brought to light was quite loose. As it tied at the sides with white cords, with another at the halter neck, this was unimportant, but gave quite a boost to her drooping morale. The result in the mirror wasn't bad at all, she thought cheerfully. The brief, white-dotted brown triangles covered her reasonably adequately, but she put her gingham shirt on top to go downstairs.

Julia was gathering up her bag preparatory for departure.

'I must dash down to Lucy Armitage's, Natalie, while you wallow in the garden. She's doing the costumes and had everyone round for a fitting yesterday while Nick and I were painting, so I promised to go through them and approve them officially this morning over coffee.'

'I thought she threw pots and things for that smart place in Stratford; the one that sells them for exorbitant prices to the tourists,' said Natalie in surprise.

'She does. But she tentatively offered to lend a hand with the costumes and turns out to be an absolute genius for inventing the unusual. I mean, you wouldn't want her to make you a tailored suit, but when it comes to strange, floating fairylike confections she's absolutely inspired. Normally she's a very shy, withdrawn person, but this has really brought her out to mix more. Did you know her name is really Lucrece, but she prefers Lucy.'

'Sensible lady!'

'Now don't stay out in the sun too long, wear your dark glasses and make yourself whatever drinks you want.'

'Yes, Mother; I'm perfectly able to cope. Do you want me to move my car?'

'No, thanks, darling, I'll walk.' Julia reached up and gave Natalie a brief kiss. 'It's only a mile or so. See you later.'

Natalie watched her mother walking purposefully down the hill from the window in the bathroom where she was searching for some sun cream, then she had a look through the bookshelves in her room and eventually decided on *Gone with the Wind* and *Anna Karenina*. Armed against boredom, she settled on the comfortable mattress of the padded lounger and felt no inclination to read at all. She went into the house and fetched the small radio instead, pleased to find Radio Three was putting out a performance of *Scheherezade*. Contentedly relaxed, she lay in the warm sunlight, the music playing softly. Unmoving, she drifted into a pleasant hazy state of suspension, where thought became superfluous, and the only thing necessary was to feel the sun on her skin and listen to the music of Rimsky-Korsakov growing fainter and fainter as she slid gradually into sleep.

As she surfaced out of a sweet, blank well of nothingness, sensations began to form into a dream. Unresisting, she gave herself up to insidious hands that slid round her and held her to a warm, hard chest. Blissfully she floated in a sweet, comforting dream, sighing unconsciously as a masculine mouth came down on hers very gently, so gently she was hardly aware of the pressure of the lips increasing gradually on hers until her own opened naturally to the demand of the mouth in her dream. Abruptly she was awake, fully. Her eyelids flew open and she stared in confusion, and then anger, at the eyes looking down into hers with mockery. Grey-green eyes with a distinctive dark rim around the iris held hers in an intent, disturbing look that was all too familiar.

Natalie sat up with a jerk, pushing violently at the arms that held her, glaring at Nick Marlowe with dislike and resentment, her temper at boiling point.

'That was just slightly underhand!' she snapped, hastily checking on her bikini top and looking round wildly for her shirt.

Nick sat back on his heels, grinning unrepentantly as he handed her the checked shirt lying on the grass behind him.

'This what you're looking for?'

'Thanks,' said Natalie tightly, pulling it on swiftly. 'Mother isn't here.'

'I know. I saw her in the village on the way to Lucy Armitage's, so I thought I'd come and beg a cup of coffee from you.'

'Did she say what I was doing?' demanded Natalie, her eyes sparkling in militant suspicion.

'No, she didn't. That was an unexpected bonus.' Nick ran a negligent, insultingly familiar finger down her bare arm. 'I was just naturally anxious about all that beautiful skin getting burned, so I thought it best to wake you up.'

'You could have chosen some other method.' Thoroughly put out, Natalie slapped away the questing finger and tried to find her sandals.

'Once I saw you lying there, like the Sleeping Beauty incarnate, all power of choice vanished.' Nick laid a hand satirically on his heart. 'I refuse to apologise. To say I'm sorry would be blatantly untrue.'

He was openly laughing at her now, but Natalie was far from amused.

'I thought I was dreaming,' she said repressively, and stalked towards the house.

'No doubt you imagined it was someone else.' He caught up with her relentlessly.

'No,' said Natalie, habitually honest, 'I just thought it was a dream. Now let's drop the subject. I suppose I'd better make you your coffee—had they run out at the Copper Kettle in the village?'

Nick lounged into the kitchen after her and sat on the table, watching her every move with disconcerting attention as she filled the percolator.

'No idea. I just wanted your company while I was drinking it. I'm a very direct, uncomplicated sort of fellow, sweetheart.'

'You don't say.' Natalie was sceptical as she sat down to wait for the percolator. In the clear bright morning light the scar on Nick's forehead stood out angry and red, and he became restive under the forthright gaze she fixed on his face, his mouth twisting in wry deprecation.

'I suppose you find it highly repellent?'

'Not particularly.'

'Just not particularly?'

'What more do you want? Embroidery? I'm a fairly direct sort of person, too. To be frank, Mr Marlowe, I don't give tuppence for your scar. What I *do* find repellent, I must admit, is the memory of our last encounter, no doubt long forgotten by you, but at the moment all too depressingly clear in my own mind.'

Natalie jumped up to pour out two mugs of coffee, then sat down again, avoiding Nick's eye while both were silent for a moment, looking back down the years to two different mental images.

'You were a sweet, engaging innocent,' said Nick bleakly. 'I was sorely tempted by your ingenuous offer, I can assure you, if only momentarily, and I really did try to let you down lightly, but obviously I didn't succeed and upset you badly.'

Natalie brushed back an unruly lock of hair and smiled at him brightly.

'Actually, Nick, to be perfectly honest, I hadn't given you a thought in years, it was so long ago. Yesterday just happened to be an extraordinarily inappropriate time to meet up with you again, that's all. I'd just been summarily disengaged, as it were, then finding you here right on top of it was too much. I could have spat in your unsuspecting eye.'

The man opposite her took her by surprise by stretching out a hand and taking one of hers.

'The man must be a lunatic! What possible reason did he have?'

'The best one there is. He found someone else he liked better.'

'Were you living together?'

Natalie snatched her hand away abruptly, incensed.

'What earthly business is that of yours?'

'None—I'm sorry, it just slipped out. For Pete's sake don't ice up again.'

He sprang to his feet and caught her arm as she was about to leave the room. Natalie looked pointedly down at his detaining hand until he removed it, then looked deliberately up into his eyes.

'Just for the records, Mr Marlowe, I share a flat with a staff nurse at the Charing Cross Hospital. I belong to that dying breed of female, the one who wishes to share a home with a man only if she marries him—which possibility at the moment seems decidedly remote. So may I ask you to leave now, please, as I need to change for lunch.'

Nick stood aside immediately, his eyes mocking and hard, and gave a slight bow.

'Thanks for the coffee, *Miss* Ross, that, at least was very enjoyable.' He strolled indolently to the kitchen door, then paused, looking at her sardonically as she stood poised for retreat. 'For the record, however, I must admit I enjoyed the appetizer before it even more—inexpert perhaps even now, but very sweet.'

With a negligent salute he took himself off, leaving Natalie brimming with impotent fury. She flew upstairs and washed her face violently with cold water in an effort to cool down, then changed back into the jeans she'd worn earlier. She lingered as long as possible over the process, her mind preoccupied disturbingly by the rather troubling little episode in the garden. For someone stricken over the ending of one so-called love affair she rather felt it was a distressingly shallow nature that could respond quite so quickly to another man's lovemaking. You thought you were dreaming, she told herself fiercely, tying back her hair ruthlessly with the nearest thing she could find, a white shoelace from an old tennis shoe. With relief she heard her mother arrive and went downstairs to join in the preparations for their lunch.

'Mr Podbury, the carpenter is coming with his lorry after lunch,' said Julia while they ate. 'He's kindly offered to move the flats over to Arden House before rehearsal. By the way, I met Nick in the village. I asked him to lunch if he would like to. Something must have come up.'

'He came for coffee instead.'

Something in Natalie's dismissive tone put Julia off talking any further on the subject, and by the time the lunch dishes had been cleared away a large man in white overalls and flat cap was tapping at the open door. Julia beamed at him.

'Hello, Mr Podbury. This is really very kind of you—you remember my daughter Natalie, of course?'

After greetings had been exchanged Natalie helped manoeuvre the flats down the path and into the lorry, panting with her exertions by the time Mr Podbury had them settled to his satisfaction for the short journey to Arden House. After a cursory glance at herself in the mirror she set off with her mother for the same destination, reluctant to chance seeing Nick again so soon, but reluctant to disappoint Julia by remaining at home.

Natalie's stomach muscles contracted as she walked along the all too familiar path through the box hedges, averting her eyes resolutely as they passed the familiar elm tree, glad when they reached Arden House. It was a solid, compact building, not over-large, built of the beautiful local honey-coloured stone, softened by creepers here and there, mullioned windows glinting through them in the sun. The tennis court was slightly to the left of the house, where the lawn sloped away, so that it lay in a natural, shallow amphitheatre. Nearest the house a broad terrace looked down on the court, with a small pool with an old disused fountain where a stone cherub held a conch shell from which presumably water had once cascaded. This terrace was intended as the stage, giving an admirable view to the audience seated on the flat court, and to others who could perch on the natural shelving bank rising on the other three sides.

Already many of the cast were gathered on the terrace, children—presumably would-be fairies—were running riot all over the place, while several men helped Mr Podbury manipulate the scenery, hastily receiving directions from Julia as she hurried over to them. Julia noted the juvenile rampage with a darkling eye and raised her voice in authority.

'Now then, fairies, a little less noise, and absolutely no more running about, please. This is Mr Marlowe's garden and he is being extremely kind to allow us to use it, so please treat it with respect. I know it's Saturday, and you're all super to give up a lovely sunny day to rehearse, but we have only one more week to the performance, so I suggest you keep your energy for working hard, not fighting. No pea-shooters, please, Nigel—Adam, stop pulling Emma's hair, dear. Thank you.'

She subsided into a small folding chair, relative peace restored, and waved Natalie to another alongside her.

'You sounded just like Joyce Grenfell, Mother,' said the latter, relaxing now that she was sure there was no sign of Nick.

'More like a regimental sergeant-major on occasion! Ah, here comes young Edgar, my stage manager.'

A thin young man of about eighteen came hurrying across the lawn, dressed in the inevitable jeans and sweatshirt, short dark curly hair cut close to his head. His eyes were filled with eager interest as he caught sight of Natalie.

'Hello, Mrs Ross, hello, Natalie,' he said shyly, 'nice to see you.'

'Edgar Holmes—hello. I didn't recognise you.' Natalie held out her hand with a friendly smile. 'I hear your uncle is a smash playing Bottom.'

He grinned as he squatted down alongside Julia.

'He is, but some of the ladies in the congregation feel the Vicar's losing his dignity by playing the fool. Only the fact that it's Shakespeare is redeeming his fall from grace.'

'They'll be surging in to fill the front row, don't you worry,' laughed Julia. 'Now how are things. Any problems?' She broke off to direct the scene-shifters. 'Could you make the arrangement of potted plants more haphazard, Mr Podbury, please? It's a tiny bit Kew Gardens like that—it's supposed to give the effect of a wood near Athens, dear. Yes—yes, that's perfect. Thank you.'

She sat back as her instructions were carried out to her satisfaction.

'Now then, Edgar—I know everyone went round to Lucy's yesterday. I approved the costumes this morning; was everybody happy?'

'Oberon's not,' said the boy gloomily.

'Why?'

'He says being the king of the fairies is enough of a burden to bear without having to wear that wig. Sam says he feels like Danny LaRue. Can he just wear his own hair?'

Julia mused a little.

'I suppose so. He can have a gilded leather thong round his forehead and we'll gild the spear he's carrying—is he happy about the leather breechclout?'

'Not very,' admitted Edgar. 'There's quite a lot of Sam, Mrs R., but I expect he won't feel so selfconscious when the others are all dressed up as well. He's pretty tanned, luckily, working stripped off down in Long Meadow.'

'Good. Now how about Titania? On the first fitting Lucy had quite a battle with her.'

'What was Titania's problem?' Natalie was riveted.

'She wanted a great deal too much cleavage and a rather too generous display of thigh. We compromised with the promise of gilded finger and toe nails and gold dust in her hair.'

'She didn't turn up yesterday, Mrs R., but she may have since. Puck was a bit bothered about the light in his hair, though.'

'The what?' asked Natalie, laughing.

'He has a mass of black curls, our Kevin,' explained Julia, 'and I thought it would be a good idea to have a tiny torch hidden in his hair, with a fine flex running down his arm to a switch in his hand that he can operate now and then. Sort of glow-worm effect.'

'Good heavens!'

'He thinks he'll electrocute himself because his hand gets sweaty when he's nervous,' explained Edgar, worry lines, engraved on his young forehead.

'Kevin doesn't possess nerves,' said Julia dismissively, 'he merely plays on other people's. Tell him to have a tissue handy. Now is everyone ready?'

While she sprang up to count heads a tanned, auburn-haired young giant strolled over to Natalie and smiled diffidently.

'Hello, Miss Ross, do you remember me?'

'Well, Sam Wyatt! Heavens, you've grown a bit since we were eleven!'

He laughed, the easy colour rising beneath his coppery, suntanned skin.

'At the risk of seeming rude I might say the same of you, Miss Ross.'

'For heaven's sake call me Natalie. As we were both puny little eleven-year-olds we must have suffered the same hormone outburst during our teens.'

Sam glanced over at Julia Ross and then back to Natalie, grinning.

'You must take after your father!'

'I wish he'd passed on his brain instead,' said Natalie gaily, 'I'd have preferred to be slightly on the daintier side like Mother and Cordelia.'

It was obvious from his attitude that Sam saw nothing the least bit wrong with her the way she was, and Natalie was quite relieved to see her mother waving them over to a group of rather stricken-looking would-be thespians. Julia looked decidedly depressed, and was fending off worried enquiries from all sides.

A chill feeling of impending doom settled between Natalie's shoulder-blades as her mother's eye caught hers with a determined gleam.

'What's wrong, Mrs Ross?' asked Sam, before Natalie could speak.

'Melanie Dalton went riding this morning, her horse threw her and she's laid up with a broken leg.'

'What happened to the horse?' asked Sam with professional interest.

'No one has seen fit to issue a bulletin on the animal,' said Julia acidly, 'so one presumes it's well. The trouble from our point of view is that we have no Titania.'

There was a resumption of the dismayed hubbub, one little girl bursting into noisy tears at the prospect of her short-lived stage career being prematurely terminated.

'No understudy, Mother?' asked Natalie.

'No. We'd had trouble enough in finding the requisite number of talented players to fill the roles as it is. I almost had to use physical force to persuade Sam here.'

A ripple of amusement ran through the crowd at

this, lifting the gloom slightly. Then Julia turned to Natalie.

'You played Titania in school, Natalie, would *you* do it? You could easily learn the lines again; it's a shortened form, and you are on holiday. Please!'

Natalie looked down into her mother's face, her heart sinking. The thought of someone her height playing the fairy queen gave her silent hysterics, but on the other hand, to be just, her mother seldom asked anything of her at all.

Natalie thought rapidly for a moment, oblivious of the sea of hopeful faces surrounding her. After all, it might not be a bad thing to be fully occupied for a while. It would help take her mind off Edward's defection for one thing; the other half-formed reason she was unwilling to admit, even to herself. If she were up to her ears in performing Titania there was considerably less chance of doing something stupid all over again as far as Nick Marlowe was concerned—the first brush with him had been sheer inexperience; a second would be sheer carelessness.

She took a deep breath and smiled.

'Very well. If you're really stuck, I'll have a shot at it.'

Everyone crowded round in jubilation and approval while Julia reached up to kiss her daughter lovingly.

'Thank you, darling,' she said quietly, a deep glow of gratitude in her eyes, 'thank you very much.'

CHAPTER FOUR

FOR an isolated moment Natalie's brain divided into two distinct halves. One of them registered her mother's gratitude and relief with warm, almost smug self-approval; the other recoiled, aghast at the rash statement her tongue had just uttered, urging it to retract before the impulsive offer could be accepted. The two halves clicked together abruptly as Puck expressed his feelings with a great yell of delight, turning cartwheels to demonstrate his relief, to the detriment of several small would-be fairies in his vicinity. There was a concerted rush as everyone pressed close to express fervent thanks and Sam Wyatt almost cut off the circulation in one of Natalie's hands with the strength of his approving clasp, his attitude altogether too proprietorial for comfort. The Vicar, arriving late on the scene just in time to hear the news, pushed his way through the excited crowd to Mrs Ross and Natalie, kissing the latter's cheek jovially.

'Blessings, my child,' he said, eyes twinkling, 'you'll get your reward in heaven, Natalie.'

'I'm happy to hear it.' Her voice was faint as an acute sensation of claustrophobia threatened to overwhelm her as she stood, hemmed in, stifled by all the unlooked-for attention suddenly thrust upon her. The sound of a familiar voice behind her had never been so thankfully welcome.

'Good afternoon, everyone, welcome to Arden House. I'm Nicholas Marlowe.'

At that precise moment he seemed to Natalie more like St George and Superman all rolled into one as the centre of interest shifted immediately from her own reluctant figure to that of the tall, tanned man in the navy shirt and white sailcloth jeans, his eye-catching scar standing out on his forehead. Nick drew Natalie close with an arm round her waist, and kept her there throughout all the introductions, to Sam Wyatt's rather obvious annoyance, not to mention the keen interest of everyone else. He quickly made himself known to everyone, having a quick word here and there, charming the teenagers, teasing the children and joking with the men playing the workmen, most of whom were already known to him. In the breathing space Nick won for her Natalie was able to recover gradually from the sudden panic of finding herself about to tread the boards, or in this case the turf, at rather alarmingly short notice.

Breaking up the social niceties, Julia marshalled everyone firmly off into their places with the intention of rehearsing all the scenes without Titania for that day, to give Natalie some time to get used to the idea.

Much to the obvious disappointment of Sam and young Edgar, Nick suggested Natalie went up to the house to have a cup of tea while he looked out an extra copy of the script he'd condensed. Julia approved promptly, obviously agreeing that her daughter needed a little breathing space. Silently Natalie allowed herself to be led up the terrace into the cool gloom of the panelled hall, her gratitude for Nick's intervention evaporated now that they were alone together.

'There's really no need for the tea,' she said distantly, avoiding his eye. 'If you'll just provide me with the necessary copy I think I'd better get back to the others.'

He shot her a hostile look, standing four square in front of her, hands thrust into the pockets of his jeans.

'Perhaps I should make it clear that Mrs Corby is in the kitchen, Natalie, so I'm unlikely to give way to my baser instincts and throw you on the parquet floor with a view to ravishing you while the kettle boils.'

Hot flooding colour rushed into Natalie's face and she turned on her heel in disgust, her whole instinct escape, but was held fast by a long hard hand on her elbow. She was forced to turn and face him while his other hand turned her reluctant face up to his. They stared at each other in baleful silence for a moment.

'Natalie, go into the drawing room for a few minutes to get your breath back, and stop being so obstinate. I'll leave you in peace and Mrs Corby will bring you the tea. Will that suit you?'

Nick's voice was deadly soft, and Natalie swallowed hard before nodding assent. He released her to open the drawing room door, then running an exasperated hand through his hair he went back through the hall to the kitchen without a word.

Natalie subsided limply on the shabby brocade of one of the sofas in the faded glory of the large room, feeling flattened, not so much by the prospect of her sudden promotion to the role of Titania, as by the underlying cut and thrust of each encounter with Nick Marlowe. No doubt she would manage the acting bit with fair efficiency, but somehow she would have to cool it in regard to her reactions to Nick. Where was all her much vaunted, sensible self-possession at the moment? she chided herself crossly. Just be ordinary, friendly, above all calm when he's around. And around he was obviously going to be during the next week or so, so she would have to pull herself together, stat. She looked up sharply as the door opened, but it was Mrs Corby with the tea-tray. The portly little woman set it down in front of Natalie on a small oak table and stood back, smiling.

'So you're going to be in the theatricals, Mr Marlowe says.'

'I must be out of my mind,' said Natalie ruefully, pouring out tea with a sigh. 'Will you have some?'

'No, thanks, dear, I'm just setting out some cold drinks for when the others have a break, those children will be thirsty in this heat. One thing I must say, you'll make a better job of Shakespeare than that young Melanie. Too full of herself by half, that young woman.'

She bustled off energetically, leaving Natalie to drink her tea and swiftly return to a more peaceful state of mind, to the point where she was able to smile politely when Nick returned.

'Having second thoughts about treading the boards, Nat?' he asked.

'I could hardly say no!'

'I know. You're a brick to take it on. Your mother would have been sunk if not, all those little dears out there would have been inconsolable, and the church tower would no doubt have collapsed completely. Besides, don't worry, you'll be "a most auspicious star".'

'Wrong play.' Natalie leaned back, then winced as the forgotten shoelace in her hair caught in the frayed edge of the sofa-cushion.

'Let me.' Nick bent over her and slid his fingers through her hair to disentangle the lace, his face very near hers, frowning and intent as he undid the knot, stiffening as she instinctively recoiled from the touch of his hand on her neck.

'There!' Natalie's hair fell loose and he straightened, moving away from her ostentatiously, an acid smile twisting his mouth. 'You'll make a ravishing Titania, have no fears.'

She looked down into her cup, flushing, but her sense of humour began to reassert itself.

'At least Oberon and I will be extremely visible to the audience, if nothing else. We'll stand out from the rest of the cast like lighthouses! Did you know Sam's costume consists merely of a leather breechclout and a gilded spear? Heaven knows what my darling parent has in mind for me.'

'A great deal more than that, I trust. We don't want the male population of Arden-under-Hill on the rampage.'

Something in Nick's dry tone made Natalie acutely selfconscious, and she sat up straight, reaching for her cup of tea.

'Don't be silly,' she said primly.

He looked at her, shaking his head in amazement.

'Have you really no idea at all how attractive you are, Natalie? Young Wyatt is out there at this very moment probably planning several different ways to cut me out, and even young Edgar has a decidedly moonstruck expression every time he looks at you, which seems to be most of the time.'

Natalie frowned and looked away from the penetrating grey-green eyes, thoroughly discomfited.

'I know I'm not bad-looking. It's just that I'm on such a large scale.'

Nick snorted with laughter, pushing his thick fair hair back from his forehead and looking her frankly up and down, sending the colour rushing back to her face yet again.

'Rubbish. How tall are you?'

'Five foot ten. Barefoot.'

'So what? Sam Wyatt is heaven knows how much more than that, so shut up about too tall—it doesn't matter a damn.'

He turned impatiently at a hesitant knock on the door, then smiled reassuringly as Edgar Holmes popped his head round it apologetically.

'Sorry to interrupt, but your mother asked would you read your scenes with the fairies, Natalie. She'd like you to get the feel of the play a little today if you've got your breath back.'

'On my way!' Natalie sprang to her feet with alacrity, taking her copy of the script from Nick. She hurried after Edgar with a brief word of thanks, leaving the man to stand watching her from the window as she ran down the terrace and joined the others. Nick opened his hand to find a frayed white shoelace lying in his palm and put it carefully in his pocket, a smile lifting a corner of his mouth, but not reaching the absent gleam in his eyes.

By six-thirty that evening all the cast, not to mention the producer, were more than glad to call it a day, voicing reiterated thanks to their host as they left for home. Nick strolled back towards Hill Cottage with Julia and Natalie through the perfect June evening.

'It was rather a nasty shock to find my Titania was in plaster,' said Julia. 'Have you forgiven me for railroading you into the part, Natalie? I did rather use moral blackmail.'

'No, I haven't. It will probably be months before diplomatic relations are resumed!'

'I do sympathise, darling, but I didn't know where to turn; and you *have* played the part before.'

'Yes, but I was about half my present size then . . .'
began Natalie, before Nick interrupted her scathingly.

'Not that old warhorse again, surely!'

'Sorry if I'm boring you!' Natalie snapped.

Julia intervened hastily.

'Personally I've always longed to be tall, so much
more elegant. Why you're so selfconscious about it I'll
never know.' Then she spoiled it by adding, 'Unless it
was the fact that Edward was the same height—
practically.'

'Oh, Mother! You never trouble about being sensitive
and tactful, do you?' sighed Natalie despairingly.

'Only when necessary. Are you coming for a drink,
Nick?'

'I promised to go back and help Mr Podbury put
polythene sheeting over those flats. I'll hold you to a
drink another time.' Nick paused, looking in direct
challenge at Natalie, although he went on addressing
Julia. 'Would you object if I took your daughter out to
dinner this evening?'

'*I* wouldn't, not in the slightest,' said Julia promptly,
avoiding Natalie's eye. 'I'm going to Lucy's to give a
hand with finishing the costumes this evening anyway.
Enjoy yourselves—I'm off to have a long, leisurely cool
bath, with my new novel and a very long drink.'

She smiled at them both serenely and went indoors.

'Shouldn't you have asked me?' Natalie turned on
Nick immediately, annoyed at his high-handed assump-
tion of her consent.

He stood, arms folded, looking at her judiciously.

'You'd have said no.'

'How do you know?'

'Because you feel it would be vaguely indecent to
consort with another man when really you should be
wailing all alone, covered with sackcloth and ashes in
mourning for your lost, lamented love,' he answered
promptly.

Natalie looked mutinously at the tall figure,
silhouetted against the evening sky, his expression
hidden from her.

'Racing driver, novelist, psychiatrist, Lord of the

Manor—are there any other faces to your personality likely to emerge, I wonder?' she said in mock deference.

'Come out with me this evening and find out.'

'Where?'

'We could just drive slowly down some minor roads and see what the Cotswolds yield in the way of entertainment, if that appeals.'

'An offer I can hardly refuse. Why not, as long as we're not too late. Thank you,' she added, somewhat belatedly.

Nick grinned at her lopsidedly.

'I thought for a moment the answer would be no.'

'Why should it?' Natalie was deliberately careless. 'You know the old song, "Saturday Night is the Loneliest Night of the Week". I shall be very glad to have company.'

'Even mine?'

'Even yours. What time? Eightish?'

'Fine. I'll bring the car up the hill to the front of the house; see you, Nat.'

With a casual nod of farewell Nick strolled unhurriedly back along the tree-lined path, leaving Natalie to stand watching him for a moment, frowning, before wandering down the garden path to the cottage, pausing to drink in the scent of the roses for a moment. What was she getting herself into now? she wondered. Nick had been uncannily accurate about her misgivings, it was only fair to admit. She *had* felt the very definite stirrings of guilt at agreeing to dine with him at all, considering how very recently, indecently so, she had felt shattered at Edward's desertion. But then Nick was more in the nature of an old friend, after all. She stopped short suddenly in her self-assurances. Oh yeah, who do you think you're fooling, Natalie? She shrugged and went in the house to choose something to wear.

Julia called from the bathroom as Natalie went up the stairs.

'Come in for a minute. I'm reasonably respectable.'

Natalie pushed open the door and laughed at the sight of her mother lying practically prone in the tub, completely obscured by a thick layer of bubbles, a frilly green bathcap on her head and a glass of what looked like lime-juice in her hand. Julia eyed her daughter with caution.

'Not too annoyed, really, are you, darling?'

Natalie subsided on to the little cork-covered stool, yawning widely.

'Why should I be? I'm looking forward to roaming round the Cotswolds in search of dinner—or at least I will be after a decent interval.'

'I wasn't referring to your evening, actually, I meant being stampeded into playing Titania.' Julia smiled into her drink. 'Obviously you're quite calm and unmoved at your sudden impending star status.'

'I don't know that I go along with that entirely. I came home to relax and lick my wounds, you know. How come I overlooked the fact that wherever you are, Mother dear, one is fortunate to sit still and take a breath, let alone relax!'

'Oh, darling, I wouldn't say that,' protested Julia.

'I would. Don't worry, I'll survive. It isn't as though the village will be expecting Maggie Smith or Judi Dench! Besides, I'm sure it will be great fun and very therapeutic for me; though I'd better start swotting up lines right away. In fact I can make a start in the bath— I'll give you fifteen minutes. What exactly is in that innocuous-looking glass?'

'Vodka and lime.' A blissful expression spread over Julia's face as she took a long swallow and closed her eyes.

'You wicked little woman!' Natalie got up, smiling. 'I'll take myself off to look at what there is to wear. Fifteen minutes, mind!'

'Wear the violet dress,' said Julia, without opening her eyes.

'Maybe. I haven't really anything to wear on my feet, at least nothing suitable.'

'Those flat gold sandals.'

'M'm—then I'll have Nick boring on about my height phobia all night.'

Julia opened one eye.

'Does it matter?'

'No, love, not a bit,' Natalie laughed, and left her mother to wallow in peace.

CHAPTER FIVE

AFTER Julia had set off for Lucy's, Natalie lay in the bath, a copy of the playlet in front of her, bullying her mind to concentrate on the familiar lines. Severe doubts about her own sanity began to stab at her. What on earth had made her agree to spend the evening with Nick Marlowe? she thought in disgust, abandoning any pretence of memorising and hurling the script away from her in exasperation. For that matter, why had Nick asked her? Boredom, no doubt, thought Natalie cynically. Maybe all those lovelies who clustered round him once were no longer interested now he'd deserted the role of glamour boy of the racing world.

Mechanically she began to soap herself, her eyes blank and inward gazing as she berated herself for a fool. She must be mad to agree to pass the time away for him for lack of anyone more exciting down here in the depths of Warwickshire. His face rose before her, something in his expression both eluding and disturbing her. He looked different from the Nick engraved in perpetuity on her memory as she had seen him last, through a veil of youthful, bitter tears. Granted the addition of seven years to his age, Nick's present expression held an oddly empty, bitter look behind the easy charm of his smile. Possibly it was the scar that caused the difference. Natalie shrugged and stood up to pat herself dry. Whatever it was the last thing she intended was probing beneath the surface to discover what troubled him. She had troubles enough of her own at the moment, one way and another, without involving herself in anyone else's.

The sun was setting in scarlet and gold glory later that evening when Nicholas Marlowe stopped his MGB in the courtyard of the Fosse Court Hotel. Natalie sat perfectly still for a moment, content just to look at the long, Jacobean building in sheer delight as the golden glow washed its honey-coloured stone with light.

'What a heavenly place, Nick—have you been here before?'

'Once for lunch. I thought of it after I asked you to eat with me, so I rang through and booked.'

She looked at him, amused.

'So all that meandering through those country lanes was just a front!'

'I thought you'd appreciate a surprise.'

Nick leaned over and undid her seatbelt, then got out to open the door for her, looking quite overpoweringly attractive in a lightweight dark blue suit, a white silk shirt open at the throat.

'As it's Saturday we'll have to wait a bit. They've rather squeezed us in, but by way of consolation we can have our drinks in the garden.'

He led her through the imposing front door along a low-ceilinged hall that opened directly out into a walled garden filled with the smell of orange-blossom in the cooling air. White-painted chairs and tables were dotted here and there on the manicured lawn, most of them occupied by convivial groups of people, either enjoying pre-dinner drinks or lingering over after-dinner coffee and liqueurs.

Natalie sat down in the white-painted chair Nick held out for her and looked round the garden with rapture. It looked as though nothing had changed in it for centuries. Nick smiled in satisfaction at her obvious pleasure in her surroundings.

'What will you drink, Natalie?'

'Oh, something long and cool, I think, Campari with lots of fresh orange juice and ice, please.'

Natalie watched Nick's tall, co-ordinated figure as he went inside to the bar, noting several feminine heads swivelling as he passed. Not much danger of the scar putting off the ladies, she thought, smiling secretly. She sat, relaxed, happy to look around her until Nick's return, noting with interest the old well near the entrance, screened by the ancient spreading branches of an extremely venerable tree.

Nick came back carrying a small tray and a large menu, handing her a tall glass before sitting down.

'I brought the menu myself,' he said, 'the bar is packed—good thing I booked.' He raised his glass to her and made a toast. 'To your big brown eyes, Natalie.'

'I'll drink to your complete recovery,' she countered. 'By the way, did you notice the tree and the well as you went in?'

'The tree is a mulberry, centuries old. The well is ancient too, but safely boarded up now.'

Natalie smiled in appreciation, her wariness temporarily forgotten.

'This is the most beautiful place, so incredibly peaceful. How old would you say it is!'

'Circa 1670, I believe. Around that corner in the orchard is what's reputed to be the remains of an old bear-baiting pit, and inside the hotel a lot of the rooms have four-poster beds. One bedroom is haunted, of course, and there's a priest hole.'

Natalie was enchanted. She sat with hands clasped under her chin, gazing at Nick in complete absorption, her eyes fixed on his with such rapt attention that he lost track of what he was saying and sat just looking at her in unashamed silence, one eyebrow higher than the other, as he made a leisurely examination of her dress and the face that grew watchful under his gaze.

'You look very beautiful this evening, Miss Ross, a sheer delight to the eye. I'm the envy of every man in sight.' Nick's voice was tinged with mockery as Natalie flushed slightly, though she continued to look back at him steadfastly.

'Thank you kindly, good sir, you're exceedingly good for my morale.'

'To hell with your morale, I'm just stating the obvious. That colour gives your skin the look of warm cream.'

The deliberately caressing note in the deep voice finally made Natalie's eyes drop, to his amusement, and she picked up the menu, studying with determined attention the impressive choice of edibles it offered.

'In addition to all this historic charm,' she said lightly, 'the menu appears highly tempting too.'

Nick bent his head close to hers to look at the list of dishes, and Natalie instinctively shifted a little, sitting upright. He straightened immediately, a sardonic smile on his face, his eyes cold.

'What would you like, Natalie?'

A good question, she thought. I must be afflicted with midsummer madness. She smiled at him with determined brightness.

'I don't really feel like anything hot; this weather makes me tend to stick to salads.'

'May I make a suggestion?'

'Yes, please,' she said, relieved. 'There's so much here I can't take it all in.'

Nick turned his attention to the menu with what she could have sworn was an effort.

'How about a clear consommé, followed by Scotch salmon? They serve it with a sauce that's a house speciality, and we'll have buttered new potatoes, green peas and some of your salad too, if you must. How does that appeal?'

'It sounds perfect.'

'May I get you another drink when I order?'

'No, thanks, I've had rather a surfeit of alcohol lately.'

He raised his eyebrows, but Natalie spared him the details. He was away for the shortest possible time, coming back to settle himself a little farther away at the small table.

'You weren't long,' said Natalie idly, noting with infinite pleasure the new moon that hung in the darkening sky above the syringas.

'I could hardly risk leaving you alone for long out here in the dusk—someone might spirit you away.'

Natalie laughed in disbelief.

'You're doing a marvellous job for my amour propre, Nick; absolute balm for my sore and wounded spirit.'

He shook his head at her quizzically, one eyebrow raised.

'I'm happy you're happy. But as I said before, the result is accidental. I'm stating nothing but the unvarnished truth.'

Natalie said nothing, merely smiling at him in doubt, refusing to be drawn.

'Tell your mother you should wear that dress to play Titania,' he said softly, finishing his drink.

'Not a chance. She's taken one of my dresses down to Lucy this evening for size, and they're hoping to do some kind of conversion job on the one intended for Melanie Dalton.'

'I suppose you'll have to match up with Sam, though I was very sincere when I suggested it might be better if you were covered up a bit more than he's likely to be!'

'You can rely on that, I assure you. Though Mother informs me she intends to match up little touches on both of us, gilded eyelids and fingernails—poor Sam!— and there was some talk of gold-dust in our hair, but I drew the line there. I'm a bit twitched about learning the lines in time. Of course it's only an extract from the play, or I wouldn't have entertained the idea, also we're playing the parts in our normal accents now, as I could never cope with trying for a rustic effect. I know my limitations.'

Nick frowned at her.

'You place too much emphasis on your so-called limitations altogether, Nat. They aren't nearly so numerous as you try to make out.'

'You've very kind, Nick,' she said, not looking at him.

His hand closed over hers savagely.

'I am *not* being *kind*! In fact if you mention anything more about my bolstering you up I'm likely to get very *un*kind—possibly violent!'

They were interrupted by the approach of a waiter to tell them their dinner was ready, and Nick put his arm lightly round Natalie to guide her into the softly-lit building.

They returned through the narrow flagged hall into a low-ceilinged dining room looking out on the courtyard. What looked like family portraits were hung at intervals on the walls, and the general atmosphere was that of a country house welcoming guests to a private dinner.

Natalie relaxed in the congenial atmosphere and

chattered away in a manner more reminiscent of the carefree teenager Nick had known years before than the wary, disillusioned creature of a few days ago. As they drank the excellent soup she grew confiding.

'Really, I think the main problem I had was in suppressing my romantic side and constantly struggling to conform to Edward's idea of the ideally suitable woman,' she told him.

'But that's barbarous!' Nick protested, frowning. 'Surely one loves another human being for what they actually are, not what one hopes they will become by remoulding.'

Natalie nodded vigorously.

'Oh, I agree now—but at the time I was busily deluding myself that all I wanted was to be the type of woman who liked the things Edward considered mandatory. It was a colossal effort sometimes, and living with Maggie has hardly been conducive to success. She's all for doing one's own thing with determination. If that's the wine waiter hovering, Nick, I don't think I really want any.'

He smiled in persuasion.

'Just a very innocuous sparkling white; a beginner's wine, just a gesture towards the salmon.'

'Oh, very well.' She smiled back. 'After all, I'm not driving.'

Nick's face sobered immediately.

'I promise I shall be under the limit, Natalie, I intend never to put anyone—including myself—at risk again.'

Natalie put out her hand in instant contrition.

'I'm a tactless idiot, Nick. Nothing was farther from my mind, honestly. Please forgive me.'

He covered the hand with his, smiling deep into her eyes.

'I have a strong feeling there's very little I wouldn't be able to forgive as far as you're concerned, Natalie.'

She drew her hand away as the waiter approached with the wine.

'That's a rash statement. You don't really know the adult Natalie very well.'

Nick took a sip from the small quantity offered to

him by the waiter and nodded in approval. When their glasses were filled and they were alone again he raised his to her in salute.

'It's odd, but I *feel* I know you very well. But here's a libation to placate the gods—to knowing you better.'

Oddly disturbed by his toast, Natalie touched her glass to his, then looked in anticipation at the dish of salmon cutlets surrounded by creamy sauce that was being presented to her.

Neither wanted anything further to eat after the main course, and accepted with alacrity when the garden was suggested as an appropriate place to linger over coffee.

By this time the slender moon was waning, but its distant gleam was supplemented by glass-shaded candles in cast-iron holders on the tables, giving a very intimate atmosphere.

'Here's your moonlight, proud Titania,' said Nick as they sat down, 'but not ill-met, I trust.'

'Not in the slightest.' Natalie began to pour coffee from the tray before her. 'Black or white?'

'Black and sweet, please. Can I persuade you to a liqueur?'

She shook her head.

'No, thanks. I've never been able to acquire a taste for the thick, sticky texture, and I like brandy only with a lot of something else to dilute it.'

As she stopped speaking the clock in the nearby church tower chimed ten and Natalie sighed in satisfaction.

'I've never enjoyed a meal more, Nick, not just the food, but being here in this beautiful garden. You were very clever to bring me here.'

She turned towards Nick as he leaned closer, but instead of some graceful comment his response was dry.

'British weather seldom allows one to enjoy anything out of doors, so I think it's luck that's contributed to the evening rather than expertise.'

Natalie was happy just to sit and enjoy the balmy evening, heavily scented as the dew settled on the flowers in the old herbaceous borders edging the lawn. Not many people remained out in the garden and they were virtually alone in their secluded corner. She could just see Nick's strongly marked profile, the dim light highlighting his fair hair and shining softly on his white shirt, his throat and face showing dark in contrast. His discarded jacket lay on another chair, and Natalie was becoming increasingly, if unwillingly, conscious of his physical proximity.

'Tell me what made you give up racing, Nick,' she asked, hurriedly battening down her thoughts. 'You were very dedicated to all the power and the glory of the track when you were younger.'

His face darkened. Even in the dim light she was able to see the sudden look of withdrawal.

'Am I trespassing?' Natalie asked quickly. 'Just tell me to mind my own business and we'll talk about something else.'

He shrugged, drawing patterns on the table top with the tip of one long, restless finger.

'You're not trespassing. I'll admit I refused to pass on my reasons to the media at the time, principally because they were a shade amorphous. Looking back over a period of time they were quite clear-cut in actual fact, though all I felt then was a violent disinclination ever to go near a race track again.' Nick looked up at her suddenly, the look of disillusion in his eyes making her stomach muscles contract.

'The truth of it is, Natalie, in a nutshell, I chickened out. Just when the Formula One World Championship title was within reach, just when, according to those in the know, I had it all in the hollow of my hand. For some time I'd had doubts about my frenetic life style, spending as many hours in the air as I did on the ground, never seeming to be in any one place for any appreciable length of time. The feminine adulation, the glamorous girls the press loved to emphasise—was it me the lovelies cared about, or was it the publicity, the dangerous, glamorous image? Which was it that attracted you, Natalie, when you were young and impressionable? Would Nick Marlowe, bank clerk or accountant, have made you so starry-eyed?' He laughed humourlessly, ignoring her gesture of involuntary repudiation. 'It was Monza that did it. There were only a couple of circuits to go. Guido Petroni was in the lead and I was just behind him. There was a heavy shower and the track became slippery. One minute he was there in front of me, the next instant his machine skidded into the barrier, tyres hurtling in the air like catherine wheels. I swerved to avoid him, managed it by some miracle, only to crash into the barrier in front of him. I was lucky. My car just stopped, but as I got myself out of it sharply I could see Guido was on fire. Literally. I managed to get him out somehow, and he survived—somehow. He was badly burned and injured, but after a fashion he's alive.'

Natalie sat motionless, her eyes fixed on his in horrified sympathy.

'I remember that happening,' she said huskily. 'You were quite a hero.'

'Rot,' Nick said with quiet sarcasm. 'I acted on instinct—just the way I drove. Some warped instinct of dicing with the devil made me race again shortly afterwards. I won, and decided to get out while I was still sane. I remember thinking "Why the hell am I doing this for a living—next week I could be dying". I had a reasonable amount of money to see me through while I found out if I could write. Apparently I can. The book was accepted, to my surprise—a thriller. I used the name Nick Christopher, and it enjoyed quite a success.'

'Then I've seen paperbacks by you on bookstalls,' said Natalie in surprise. 'Imagine it being you all the time!'

'Does that soften you in any way as far as I'm concerned?' he put in swiftly.

Natalie stiffened, then sat back in her chair, making herself relax.

'You mean am I going to get all flushed and impressed because you're a successful writer?'

'Not quite. I merely meant that racing obviously appeared in a frivolous light to you, and writing has more earnest, worthy connotations.' His face was bland and inscrutable as he savoured his brandy.

'Not in the least,' she protested lightly. 'I'll admit that at seventeen I thought your way of life highly glamorous, though that was by no means why I made my idiotic offer. I was dazzled, of course. . . .'

'I was well aware of that,' he interrupted, frowning into his glass.

'One changes as one grows older.'

'I'm very well aware of that, too.' Suddenly he changed the subject. 'In an attempt to impress you further I thought you'd like to know that I have an alter ego now, called Nicholas Marlowe, who writes historical novels for a rather more intellectual public— I'm in the middle of the second one—while Nick Christopher turns out popular thrillers to keep me out of the red.'

Natalie regarded him with an expression of mock awe.

'How organised can you get! Nevertheless I imagine your uncle's legacy was very welcome just the same, at least you don't have any security problem.'

'That was an incredible windfall,' he admitted. 'My father was his younger brother, of course, but both my parents died when I was relatively young, which was the reason I spent my holidays at Arden House when I was in school. Uncle disapproved violently of my racing, wanted me to be 'something in the City', so I was shown the door and asked never to darken it again when I refused to toe the line. Crotchety old so-and-so! The last thing I expected was to be left anything at all, let alone the house, and when I heard there was a money legacy as well I was dumbfounded. At first I thought I'd sell it, but after a while I decided to live there in comfort and spend a great deal more time on research; not a blessing granted to many.' He shifted in his seat to look at her more closely. 'I must be boring you out of your mind. I can't see whether your eyes are glazing over in this light.'

'Of course you're not,' Natalie said swiftly. 'I've been listening with rapt attention. I admit I've often wondered what happened to you since you gave up racing; I think you were very wise to get out when you did. It's a pity your uncle didn't soften when you started writing, especially as you must have had a very lonely boyhood, losing your parents so early in life.'

'They were quite elderly before I even arrived—I've always presumed my advent was quite a shock, as my mother was in her forties. I know they seemed very elderly compared to my friends' parents. Of course with some people age seems to have no effect at all, as in your mother's case. How is it you don't see too much of her, Natalie?'

Natalie was silent for some time before answering.

'Well,' she began slowly, 'Cordelia was at home with her when I first went away, working as a receptionist for the doctors in the village, and I didn't think my absence would be felt too badly, especially after three years away in college. I found it difficult to contemplate settling back in Arden, and had the chance of this rather high-powered job in London. Mother was all encouragement, so off I went. I was lucky to meet Maggie shortly afterwards, so I moved out of the hostel where I was living to share a flat with her. Then I met Edward, and most of the rest you know. None of us could have foreseen that Cordelia would win a competition, the prize for which was a weekend for two in Paris. She asked me to go with her, but the very first night we met Jean-Luc. It was quite amazing—I really thought such things didn't happen outside the pages of fiction, but they took one look at each other in the restaurant of the hotel, and one could almost hear the violins! I spent my weekend in Paris sightseeing alone while Cordelia and Jean-Luc passed the time in a mutual daze. She was never able to say afterwards where they went or what they saw. They were married six months later, and now, joy of joys, at last she's pregnant. They're both ecstatic, I gather.'

Natalie's voice trailed away a little on the last, and Nick jumped immediately to his feet, holding out his hand.

'Come on, Titania. Home. You need all the sleep you can get for the forthcoming crash course. How to be a smash hit in one week flat!'

Successfully diverted, Natalie smiled and went with him gladly. They were soon driving at a very leisurely pace along deserted country lanes in the heart of the Warwickshire countryside.

'Lovely county, leafy Warwickshire,' said Natalie dreamily. 'London will seem very stuffy and hot when I go back, though Chiswick is really very pleasant.'

Her companion was silent, and it was with a feeling of foreboding that she realised he was slowing down, warning bells beginning to ring in her head as he turned the car into a dark deserted layby overhung with trees. This moment had been the reason for her initial reluctance to accept his invitation, she realised in resignation. Surely Nick didn't expect to turn the clock back seven years and pick up where they'd left off beneath the branches of the elm tree at Arden House. If so he was sadly mistaken, she thought angrily; no way was he about to have dear little Natalie fall into his lap like a plum ripe for picking. It was her own fault, she should have stayed home and learnt her lines.

When Nick turned towards her in the dim light she could sense the tension in his taut, athlete's body, and all the wary amity of the past few hours disappeared dramatically. When he slid both arms round her she stiffened, pushing him away violently as she sat bolt upright.

'Is this the point where I'm expected to sing for my supper?' she asked acidly. 'Or should I say "perform"? If so, no chance, even though you went to such great expense for the meal.'

With a muttered curse Nick heaved himself back in his seat, his jaw set as he stared ahead of him through the windscreen into the dark night. He remained silent and still for so long Natalie became restive before he eventually broke the silence that was electric with suppressed emotions on both sides.

'I gave up smoking when I was in my teens,' he said conversationally after a while.

Natalie was blank, her body tense with nerves.

'How interesting.'

'It's at moments like this, when after all these years,

the urge to smoke is almost as strong as the other urges I'm doing my level best to ignore.' Nick drew a long, deep breath and turned his head towards her. Natalie stared stonily in front of her.

'I apologise, Natalie, not for what I did, which was nothing at all, but for what I wanted to do, which wasn't really so heinous a crime either,' he said coldly. 'We had a pleasant, congenial evening together, we're hardly strangers after all, and I merely wanted to hold you for a moment and kiss that beautiful mouth—which, I might add, wouldn't be for the first time. A car like this is hardly conducive to scenes of violent seduction.'

'I'm sorry you were disappointed. No, I'll take that back, I'm not sorry in the least. Perhaps it would be best if I made it quite clear that I'm just not in the market for casual dalliance.' Natalie turned her head towards him suddenly in enquiry. 'Or perhaps you thought you were doing me a kindness in providing a little physical consolation in the light of my recent mortifying experience?'

'My goodness, you needn't make it sound so damned sordid,' he said in disgust. 'No, I did *not* think you were pining for "physical consolation", I just had a normal desire to hold you in my arms and kiss you, a natural culmination to what I, at least, thought was a very enjoyable evening. Your much-valued self-possession was never for a moment at risk, I assure you.'

'Oh, that was never in doubt,' said Natalie carelessly, 'I never lose my cool.'

A long hand shot out and caught her chin, turning her face sharply towards him again.

'Never?' he asked softly, deep in his throat.

Natalie removed his hand summarily.

'No, never. Now I think I'd better get home, if you wouldn't mind—as you said earlier, I shall need to work hard for the next few days.'

Without answering he started up the car and drove home in smouldering silence at a speed that made her distinctly apprehensive, though she would have died of fright rather than ask Nick to slow down a little. As the car drew up outside Hill Cottage she began to struggle with the seat-belt, but to her annoyance she failed to find the release button and had to submit to Nick's assistance. He leaned over and undid the belt, then took her by surprise and kissed her hard, her head held immobile between two relentless hands while he laid siege to her protesting, resistant mouth until her lips finally parted, if only in an effort to breathe. Ignoring her hands, which vainly tried to push him away, he began to kiss her in earnest, his breath coming faster as her struggles increased. His arms dropped to encircle her, giving her the chance to lash out at him, catching the side of his face with a blow whose aim was due to luck rather than skill.

With a curse he jerked away from her, a hand to his cheek, and Natalie flew out of the car and up the small drive to the cottage without a backward glance.

In her fury it was a great effort for her to get herself to bed quietly, without disturbing her mother. As she undressed her mind seethed in company with her throbbing mouth. Most of the evening had been enjoyable, if with definite undercurrents at times, but she had been a fool to think Nick was likely to let it end without some sort of physical demonstration. Moron, fool! she derided herself savagely, brushing her crackling hair with violence. You could have said a polite no to the evening in the first place, stayed home and avoided any complications. She settled herself in her narrow bed, gazing out in wide-eyed wakefulness at the brilliance of the stars, luminous in the velvet June night. Her relationships with men were really a lot too unco-ordinated, she thought irritably, it would be a refreshing change to know someone who felt the same way at the same time. A disquieting little voice in the far recesses of her mind refused to be silenced, and told her remorselessly she *had* felt the same way tonight, if she were honest. It was her pride that had been so determined to rebuff Nick. Sort of tit-for-tat, really, wasn't it? sneered the disagreeable little voice.

Restlessly Natalie thumped her pillow and tried to

compose herself for sleep. When, eventually, after what seemed like hours, she finally began to feel drowsy, an unwelcome thought jerked her wide awake again.

She had struck Nick full on his newly-healed scar.

CHAPTER SIX

AFTER lying awake most of the night the dawn chorus was lost to Natalie next morning. She slept right through it, oblivious of sunrise, even of the smell of coffee and bacon floating upstairs. Eventually she stirred and stretched, glancing idly at her watch, then shot out of bed in guilt. It was ten o'clock, and a beautiful day going to waste. She washed swiftly and tied on a pink towelling robe over her brief lawn nightdress.

Julia was just coming into the kitchen with a bunch of mint as Natalie was pouring herself a cup of tea.

'I'm late,' apologised Natalie, with a guilty smile.

'Plenty of time before church,' answered her mother cheerfully.

'Do you want me to come?'

'Oh, I think so, darling, especially as the Vicar is coming to lunch.' Julia sat down to drink the tea Natalie handed her. 'Did you have a good time last night?'

'We went to the most attractive place, the Fosse Court Hotel. It was easy to picture Charles II wandering into the garden at any moment. We had a delicious meal—salmon cutlets—and drank our coffee by the light of a waning moon.' Natalie was careful to avoid details, a fact not unnoticed by her amused parent.

'Very lyrical!'

'The influence of the Immortal Bard, I expect.' Natalie frowned. 'I don't have anything very church-ish to wear, really, Mother.'

'That green affair you arrived in will do, but tie the sash round the middle, and a slip underneath might be a good idea. Shall I cook you some breakfast?'

'No, thanks,' Natalie's stomach rebelled at the thought. 'Another cup of tea and I'll get myself dressed. Why were you picking mint, by the way?'

'I'm not terribly efficient about labelling joints in the freezer. When the beef had defrosted this morning it turned out to be lamb. Never mind, possibly more suitable in this heat anyway.'

Natalie went up to her room and dressed swiftly, tying the sash round the waist of the green dress with a vicious yank. She felt oddly depressed as she applied a bare minimum of make-up and brushed her hair severely away from her face. I'm guilty because I should be depressed about Edward, when actually I think I'm rather more depressed about Nick, she thought ruefully. Nothing like coming home to recuperate from one man and finding one was still fighting a sort of rearguard action over the embers of an old love that should be cold, respectable ashes after all this time. And so it was! She would take very good care that it was, she thought with determination, securing her hair at the nape of the neck with one of its own thick strands wound round and fastened with a hairpin.

Despite her outward poise, Natalie felt uneasy as she sat beside her mother in the beautiful, ancient little church of St Luke's, the summer sun striking through the stained glass windows and shining on the patina of the dark oak pews, highlighting the gleaming brasses on the altar. All through Mr Holmes's brief but characteristically pithy sermon she felt a frisson between her shoulder blades, and was hardly surprised to find Nicholas Marlowe outside on the path as she and Julia emerged after the service ended. He stood tall and immaculate in the morning sunshine, his hair for once severely disciplined, his dark formal suit and striped shirt contrasting violently with the large plaster on his face.

'Nicholas! Good morning,' said Julia, smiling enquiringly. 'What on earth has happened to your face?'

'I rather forgot my scar when I was shaving this morning, Mrs R.,' he said, his face deadpan, then he turned to Natalie with a suave smile. 'And how are you this morning, Natalie? No hangover from last night?'

'Should I have?' she answered serenely. 'A beginner's

wine, I think you termed it, and I had only one glass, after all. I slept like a baby.'

The look in his light cold eyes was like steel as Julia turned away to talk to friends emerging from the church.

'We must do it again some time soon, Natalie.'

'Oh, I don't think so, thank you. My time will be pretty well taken up while I'm here. If you're bored with rustic peace I'm sure you can think of other ways to divert yourself.' Natalie was equally frosty, her eyes challenging him.

'It's plain that your visit to church hardly achieved a state of grace.'

'I don't agree,' said Natalie, noting with pleasure that one of his hands was slowly clenching and unclenching. She remembered vividly from the past that this augured imminent loss of the Marlowe temper, but felt happily secure in such a public, unassailable place. 'My state of mind is perfectly satisfactory—yours is of no interest to me.'

'I'll take you up on that some other time,' he said harshly, 'I can remember when everything I did and felt was of prime importance to you——' he broke off to smile and nod at several people passing.

'Ancient history,' countered Natalie, smiling sweetly. 'I'm older, and I hope wiser now. By the way, thank you so much for a delicious dinner last night. I forgot my manners when I departed so precipitately.'

Nick stared down at her broodingly, one hand fingering the plaster on his face.

'Don't you feel the slightest tinge of remorse in respect to this?'

'No,' she said flatly. 'Opportunist behaviour merits rough treatment. I don't care to be mauled.'

'At one time you used to revel in it.' The soft insinuation in his voice made her squirm as she looked over towards there her mother was chatting.

'That's a foul thing to say! I was too young and stupid to know any better, and after all, I would point out that at that time I had no scale of comparison. Now I'm a little more discriminate.'

'Brat,' he said, smiling pleasantly, his eyes murderous.

'I love you too,' cooed Natalie, sighing with relief as her mother rejoined them, then felt cold dismay when Julia promptly asked Nick to join them for lunch. He refused politely, to her intense relief, his eyes skewering hers as he explained that everything had been laid on for him at home by Mrs Corby, then he took graceful leave of them both and departed, leaving them to chat to various people until the Vicar appeared. Their lunch guest was some time before completing his after-church handshakes, but eventually the Reverend Oliver Holmes came dashing out of the vestry in his usual energetic fashion, full of apologies to both the waiting ladies.

'Very good to see you in church, Natalie,' he said, smiling slyly. 'When was the last time?'

'Much too long ago—don't make me feel guilty!' she laughed. 'Besides, if you're nasty to me I'll make sure Oberon doesn't remove the ass's head and keeps you under the spell!'

The three of them spent a pleasant lunch-hour discussing arrangements for the play. Regretfully their guest would be unable to attend rehearsals that day as it was Sunday, but Julia was expecting everyone else at Arden House later that afternoon, and intended running through her lines with Natalie before the rehearsal began at four. To her surprise the words quickly returned to Natalie, legacy from the time she had played Titania in school.

'It's not nearly as long a part as I remembered, learning it was a dreadful chore when I was in school.'

Julia and Natalie were having a quick cup of tea before embarking on the rehearsal.

'There's just the one really long speech, the rest isn't too bad.' A sudden thought struck Julia. 'There's Cordelia's old cassette player upstairs, and if there's a blank tape somewhere I think it would help if you spoke your part into it and then listened to the playback from time to time.'

'Good idea—I'll do it tonight. By the way, Mother, what's happening about my costume? One way and another I didn't get the opportunity to ask this morning.'

'Oh yes, of course, I forgot to tell you, I'm afraid Melanie's dress was useless. She's not only about six inches shorter everywhere, but a couple of inches wider, too, if not more.'

'Oh, great! Now what do we do?' Natalie looked at her mother in consternation.

'Not to worry, I had a brainwave. Do you remember those old evening dresses of mine you and Cordelia used to dress up in?'

Natalie was suspicious.

'Ye-es, but as you, Mother dear, are also inches shorter than me everywhere, I can't quite see how I'm any better off.'

'If you'll let me finish,' said Julia patiently. 'I used the beaded yellow silk one to make a sort of low, square-necked bodice, while Lucy unpicked Melanie's dress, which is in a creamy muslin type of material, and she's hung pieces of it from the bodice like handkerchiefs so that it falls in assymetrical lengths and floats in suitable fairylike manner. Also she added in a couple of pieces of gold and green satin from my old dresses, to add a note of colour as underskirts—and possibly make you reasonably decent at the same time. It's all tacked together, waiting for you to try it on. You can do that this evening.'

Natalie sat with her elbows on the kitchen table, chin in hands, looking at her mother's enthusiastic face with doubt.

'Mother, I don't want to be a wet blanket, but are you quite sure I'm not going to look remarkably like a maypole?'

'You really are exasperating!' Julia turned roundly on her offspring. 'Just as you are, at this very moment, you're a very attractive girl. By the time I've finished with you on the night of the play you'll be something to take the breath away—do you mind playing the part barefoot?' she broke off suddenly.

Natalie jumped up and gave her parent a hug and a smacking kiss.

'For you, anything, you bully! How can I refuse? Come on, your public awaits.'

From then on, in direct contrast to the rest and relaxation hoped for during her unplanned stay at home, Natalie worked harder for the next few days than she ever had in her life. Apart from learning the actual lines, she also had to learn to move gracefully enough to suit her mother's exacting requirements, to project her husky voice correctly through the microphones set up in front of the 'stage', and generally think herself into the role of ethereal, other-worldly being, not to mention standing with patience while her costume was practically created on her person by the painstaking Lucy. Generous help was given on all sides, as the others were already word-perfect, and only too ready to assist her in any way possible. Sam Wyatt, in particular, was all for going through their scenes together in private after rehearsals had finished, but Julia put a damper on this, vetoing extra rehearsals with the plea that Natalie would become overtired.

The strain of rehearsals was augmented by Nick's ever-present brooding surveillance, which seemed to be focussed on her whatever she was doing without any actual personal contact. Aware that her mother was refraining nobly from asking if anything was wrong, Natalie carried on with the job in hand, ignoring Nicholas whenever and wherever possible until Tuesday evening after rehearsal, when he wandered over to the group of players as they prepared to depart. Natalie was engaged in fending off another eager offer from Sam Wyatt to run through their scenes together in private. As she opened her mouth to refuse tactfully Nick's deep, decisive voice cut in swiftly.

'I think that's overdoing it a bit, Wyatt. Natalie will get overtired if she does any extra—and as far as I can tell she seems not too far from word-perfect right now.' He looked challengingly at Natalie as he spoke, lounging against a garden seat, looking anything but owner of Arden House in faded jeans and an ancient white sweatshirt. Before Natalie could explode at his high-handed interference Julia broke in hurriedly.

'It's very kind of you, Sam—if Natalie feels she needs it later on we'll give you a shout.'

Sam's crestfallen, flushed face creased with a rueful smile as he bade them goodnight, Julia walking a little way with him to discuss one of his scenes with Puck, and pour oil on troubled waters.

'That was totally unnecessary,' said Natalie coldly, eyeing Nick with dislike.

He shrugged indolently. 'It just seemed to me you're run off your feet already. There are huge dark shadows under your eyes and you look fagged out.'

'Thanks,' she said shortly. 'I'm perfectly all right; enjoying it all enormously, in fact.'

He pushed himself away from the seat and moved closer, his eyes wintry as he noted her instinctive retreat.

'For Pete's sake, Natalie, I'm not going to leap on you out here in public, or anywhere else for that matter.'

'I didn't think you were.' She looked over her shoulder, relieved to see her mother returning. 'Sam wasn't offended, was he, Mother?'

'No, of course not. A bit over-eager, that's all. He has such a splendid constitution he imagines everyone else is capable of the same.' Julia turned to Nick with a smile. 'How about sharing pot luck with us, Nicholas?'

Natalie was sure he would refuse, but to her chagrin he grinned disarmingly and accepted, turning to walk with them through the blue and gold evening in the direction of Hill Cottage. Natalie strolled in silence, leaving the other two to discuss the progress of the play. He might have had the decency to refuse, she thought, fuming; really her mother was inclined to be a little shortsighted on occasion. Surely it was obvious that relations between Nick and herself were strained, to say the least. In apparent blithe disregard of any awkwardness Julia chattered on, Nick listening with undivided attention while Natalie wondered wearily how long he was likely to stay. The last thing she felt like tonight was a meal seasoned by the verbal fencing she seemed obliged to parry whenever Nick was in the offing. *I feel like someone permanently living behind* one of those masks fencers wear, she thought, afraid to let it slip in case he cuts through my defences. I was lulled into a state of false security during Saturday evening, both by the romantic surroundings, and hearing Nick's account of his early life, then look what happened later. She had fallen a little way behind and the other two turned to wait for her at the gate to Hill Cottage.

'Nicholas insists on whipping up the meal for us,' said Julia, noting her daughter's pale, weary face with a worried frown.

'As long as you expect nothing more expert than sandwiches,' grinned Nick. 'Why don't you go and lie in the garden while I raid the kitchen cupboards?'

All at once the prospect of lying alone, prone, was wonderfully alluring, and Natalie obeyed meekly without a word while the other two went indoors to prepare the meal. Given free rein of the contents of cupboards and refrigerator, Nick forbade Julia to do anything other than set a tray and make tea. She sat down at the table in unwonted idleness and watched his preparations with interest.

'Anything Natalie detests?' he asked, buttering bread efficiently.

'No, not as far as I can remember.' Julia was silent for a time, then she looked up at Nick with anxious eyes. 'You don't think I've done the wrong thing, pushing her into village theatricals like this? At the time I thought it would be therapeutic for her in the light of—of——'

'That cretin turning her down, you mean.' Nick's voice was momentarily savage, and he sliced through a pile of sandwiches with a violence that gave the impression that they were a substitute for Edward Herrick's neck. 'I think it's been a godsend, myself. It's taken her mind off him apparently very success-fully, but it's obvious she received a blow, a major one, when he broke their engagement, and the aftermath of this, combined with all this dashing about to rehearsals and memorising her lines, is probably tiring her out no end. Personally, I'm sure it's all doing a great deal more good than sitting about brooding, so don't worry, Mrs R., all will be well.'

'I hope so. And how are you, Nick? No more headaches or dizzy spells?'

'None at all, I think I'm out of the wood. And I don't mean a wood near Athens, either!'

Julia giggled and made the tea, then they took their picnic out into the garden to join Natalie, who was fast asleep. Julia noted that there was no milk-jug on the tray and went quietly away to fetch it while Nick went down on his knees alongside Natalie. She was wearing a bright pink cotton shirt with a rather ancient button-through denim skirt, and had kicked her sandals off, as usual. She looked defenceless and young lying there, one hand trailing on the grass, the blue shadows under her eyes filling the man watching her with the urge to pick her up and hold her close. He smiled wryly at his thought and began tickling her under her chin with a blade of grass.

'Nat,' he said softly. 'Wake up, Sleeping Beauty, time to eat!'

She muttered and stirred, her eyes slowly opening to look straight up into his. For a fleeting instant a smile glowed in their dark, sleepy depths until she was fully conscious of the tanned face bending over her own, then the usual shutters came down rendering them blank. Julia reappeared, milk-jug in hand, and Natalie smiled at her in sleepy apology as she struggled to a sitting position.

'It must be this unpolluted Warwickshire air, or something, but I keep falling asleep at odd moments. I can't think what's the matter with me.'

'You were long overdue for a holiday, darling, I expect.' Julia sighed in contrition. 'I really shouldn't have pushed you into stepping in for Melanie.'

'Rubbish!' Natalie was emphatic. 'I'm enjoying myself immensely.' She caught sight of the laden tray in amusement. 'What on earth have you concocted, Nick? There's enough to feed an army!'

'I wouldn't bet on it, I'm a growing boy.' Nick selected one of each type of sandwich and put them on a plate, handing it to her with an exaggerated flourish. 'Salmon and cucumber, prawn cocktail on lettuce, ham and cheese with chives.'

Julia and Natalie were appreciative of their impromptu feast, and they sat enjoying the diminished heat of the setting sun while they ate.

'I keep worrying about the weather.' Julia looked at the blazing sunset with misgivings. 'Do you think it will really hold out until Saturday?'

'Fred Gibbins, who's painting my drawing-room, says quite definitely it will stay "fair for well nigh another week at least" yet,' said Nick comfortingly, 'and even Mother Nature would baulk at flouting one of his pronouncements, so I'm sure you'll be lucky, Mrs R.'

'I do hope so, your garden makes such a beautiful setting I must admit I'd be very disappointed if we had to move into the Village Hall now.'

'I've had an idea which I hope you'll both approve.' Nick put another sandwich on Natalie's plate. 'Yes, of course you can eat it.'

Natalie looked mutinous, but did as she was told, to her own surprise.

'What's your idea?'

'After the play I thought I'd throw a little party for the cast in my newly-decorated drawing-room; just bits and pieces to eat and plenty of beer and wine. I thought it would round off the evening.'

Both his companions regarded him with surprise and pleasure.

'Why, Nick, that would be lovely,' said Julia. 'It's always a bit of an anti-climax after any sort of amateur performance if one goes straight home when it's just a one-off occasion. I'm not sure about the children, though—the fairies, I mean.'

'I'll invite their parents,' said Nick, 'then they can take them off when they get tired.'

'I'll help make things . . .' began Natalie.

'No, you won't—thank you just the same.' Nick shook his head decisively. 'Neither of you ladies need concern yourselves with the catering. I had a tentative word with Mrs Corby and she's raring to go. I've just installed a freezer and she says she can do it all a bit at a time beforehand. Also, apparently, she has a sister-in-law who has "a light hand with pastry".'

'Oh well,' said Julia, enlightened, 'if you're lucky enough to have Doris and Ethel Corby's help you won't need our tender ministrations. Everyone enlists Ethel's help for weddings and parties. She could do with the money, too, to eke out her widow's pension.'

'Honestly, Mother,' Natalie laughed indulgently, 'I think you know all there is to know about everyone in the village!'

'Nonsense.' Julia got up and began piling dishes on the tray. 'And if I do I try to use my knowledge for the general benefit of all concerned. Absolutely no blackmail!' She waved Nick away. 'No, dear, I'm going to see to this and then watch that serial on the television. I've been following it faithfully, and tonight is the dramatic dénouement.'

Nick insisted on carrying the tray for her, then came back to sit on the grass beside Natalie's lounger, where she lay supine again, unmoving, like a rag doll. They were both silent for some time while the last rays of sunset disappeared and the shadows lengthened in the garden.

'Are you all right, Natalie?' Nick asked eventually, his eyes on the pale blur of her face, unable to make out her expression in the half light.

'Perfectly. I'm just being sinfully lazy, that's all.'

'Enjoy it while you can. I've allotted myself just one more week of lotus-eating, then it's back to the typewriter.'

'Which of your literary egos is in the driving seat at the moment?'

'Nicholas Marlowe himself. I'm having a shot at a novel encompassing the Battle of Waterloo. I know it's been done incessantly, but the period fascinates me—the characters seem to create themselves. I've been steeped in research over the thing since the accident, or at least as soon as I could read without discomfort, so now it's time to get down to the actual writing again.'

Nick looked up at her. 'How long will you stay after your glittering first—and last—night?'

Natalie sighed.

'Just another week, then back to the city. At the moment, to be honest, the prospect doesn't precisely fill me with delight. Perhaps when our economic climate improves sufficiently and jobs are easier, I might look for something in this area.'

'A long way from Covent Garden and all the attractions of the capital.' His eyes were unwaveringly intent on hers.

'Not too far away by car.' Although the dusk concealed his actual expression, something in the way Nick was looking at her made Natalie restive. 'Don't look at me like that!'

'Like what?' He edged closer.

'Like a big cat about to pounce on its helpless prey.'

He laughed softly and stretched out a hand to clasp one of hers.

'Natalie?' His face came nearer, and she shrank away on the lounger until there was nowhere to retreat without tumbling ignominiously on the grass. 'Whatever happened to my lovely, warm, impulsive seventeen-year-old?'

'She grew up, became cool and sensible—and intends to remain that way,' Natalie said levelly.

'Does that mean we have to be at daggers drawn permanently?'

'Once bitten, twice shy,' she said tartly, nettled at the mocking, indulgent note in his deep voice. 'You can hardly expect people to keep their emotions on ice until some juncture more suitable for you, Nicholas Marlowe.' She pulled her hand irritably away from his, suddenly wishing for nothing more than to be away from his disturbing presence and alone in her bed.

As if something in her withdrawal triggered off his temper, Nick sprang to his feet, stooping to pick her up bodily from the lounger. He held her there for a moment, her arms and legs flailing in anger, then lowered her abruptly to the grass and lay half on top of her, easily subduing her thrashing, struggling body by the sheer superior strength of his own. He secured both of her wrists in one long hand while his other arm held her closely against him until her impotent struggles subsided and her breathing gradually slowed.

He looked deep into the smouldering, resentful eyes so close to his own, a smile lifting one corner of his mouth while he frustrated her efforts to free herself with infuriating ease.

'It's no use, Nat,' he said caressingly. 'I've got you just where I want you, so what are you going to do about it?'

'Nothing!' she spat resentfully. 'I'll just stay here until you see fit to let me go. What possible pleasure you can find in sheer physical domination I fail to see!'

He chuckled mockingly.

'Which just proves how abysmally little you know about men, my love. Didn't you realise that the very act of physical dominance is in itself a powerful aphrodisiac? Every struggle you make only serves to fuel the flame. Just having your body close like this, however unresponsive you try to be—oh no, you don't!'

His arm tightened round her snugly and his hand clasped both of hers as she made a despairing lunge away from him.

'Let me up!' she gasped. 'Why are you doing this? Is it just to prove that Nick Marlowe still possesses his old charisma? Are you afraid the famous charm no longer works. . . .'

With a muffled curse his mouth came down on hers, cutting off her jibes midstream and rendering her helpless beneath his onslaught. When he raised his head slightly he was unmoved by the sight of tears trickling from beneath her lids and merely licked away the moisture with his tongue. Suddenly her body relaxed and he cautiously released his hold on her hands. She remained unmoving against him as his mouth came down on hers again, gently and with subtlety this time, moving over her lips while he cradled her against him with one arm, his free hand smoothing her hair, sliding over her shoulders and down her spine, moulding her still closer against him, while the pressure of his kiss hardened and became more urgent. Natalie lay still, willing herself to immunity from the mouth and hands and the hard urgent body that hotly demanded her response. Suddenly his questing hand found the summit of one breast, and the caress sent a shiver of fire through her body and made her gasp involuntarily. With a muttered sound of triumph deep in his throat Nick moved his mouth in a burning path down her throat while his clever, educated fingers wrung from her the response she was finally powerless to withhold.

Despite herself she felt her body yield and move against his. Instead of pushing him away as she instructed them, her hands crept round the back of his neck, pressing his head even closer as she wildly returned the caress of his, increasing the tempo of his breathing as tremors of excitement ran through his muscular body, communicating themselves to hers until they were both engulfed in a mutual vibrant tide of feeling.

Just when Natalie was almost lost to anything but the urgent demands of her senses she felt Nick's fingers at the buttons on her shirt. Sanity returned in full spate and she wrenched herself away from him, pulling her clothes into place and trying vainly to smooth her hair into some semblance of normality. She backed away as Nick rose slowly to his feet, looming over her in the darkness. She swallowed and turned, poised for flight, but was halted by a relentless hand on her elbow that turned her to face him, her eyes shadowed and stormy as she tried to calm herself.

'You were quite safe, Natalie!' The smug note in his voice set her teeth on edge. 'I just wanted to see how indestructible this famous cool of yours really is. It was a very instructive little experiment. I think you'll have to admit that the chemistry is still undeniably there.'

'If you're interested in chemistry and experiments, fine,' she snapped. 'Myself I'm not. Now if you'll excuse me I'd like to go into the house.'

'Besides,' he went on, ignoring her interruption, 'I trust I have better manners than to seduce my hostess's daughter on her own lawn.'

Natalie stood rigid with rage.

'Always supposing said daughter would have allowed you the privilege!'

'The other thing, Natalie Ross, is that when I do make love to you, I want you completely alive, warm, responsive and ardent in my arms. Tonight you're overtired and strung up. I would have been what's commonly known as "taking advantage of you".'

'I don't care for your choice of conjunctions—if that's the right part of speech, Mr Novelist.' Natalie's voice dripped ice. 'Would it not be more graceful to say "if" you make love to me, not "when"?'

Instead of answering he jerked her roughly into his arms and kissed her in a manner so explicit she struggled frantically, trying desperately to free herself from arms like steel bands. He lifted his head the merest fraction and looked down into the pale blur of her face.

'It's useless to fight the inevitable, Natalie. One day soon we *shall* make love. It's an inescapable fact. I mean to have you, and you can accustom yourself to it as soon as you like—and I don't recommend trying to stop me again.'

Natalie wrenched herself away, breathing hard and trembling with fury.

'And if I don't like?'

'Ah, but you do, or at least if you don't I shall soon be able to make you.'

The utter certainty in Nick's deep voice flicked Natalie on the raw—so much so she turned away blindly into the house. The television serial was just ending, and Julia looked up with an abstracted smile as Natalie almost ran into the room, followed more slowly by Nick.

'The final episode was a bit of an anti-climax after all,' she said, switching off the set, 'and as usual there was far too much emphasis on sex.'

'Isn't there always?' murmured Natalie, settling herself on the chintz-covered settee with a sigh.

Ignoring this Nick bent and kissed Julia's cheek.

'Goodnight, Mrs R., I think you should both turn in fairly soon. No doubt you'll both be up to your ears in Shakespeare again tomorrow.'

'I expect you're heartily sick of the uproar already, Nick. You'll be relieved when it's all over and Arden House is peaceful again.'

'Not in the least. In any case, I'm off to London for a couple of days to combine a spot of research with a trip to my publishers. I usually beg a bed for the night with an old friend from college days, so I shan't see you for a while. Don't work too hard, both of you.'

Nick stood looking down sombrely at Natalie, who avoided his eye as she smiled politely.

'Have a good trip, drive carefully.'

'I'm afraid I don't drive that far yet. Mrs Corby's husband is running me to Coventry to catch an early train.'

'That's a relief,' said Julia warmly, then hesitated as Natalie made no move. 'I'll see you to the door, dear.'

Nick waited a moment longer, then said quietly,

'Goodnight, Natalie, I hope you feel more lively tomorrow.'

She stared up at him without expression.

'I'm sure I shall. Goodnight.'

He stood looking down at her stonily for a moment longer, then followed Julia out through the back of the house.

Natalie sat looking down at her bare feet in vexation. Her sandals lay abandoned in the garden due to Nick's overbearing behaviour, but she would wait until he was long gone before collecting them. Julia was some time before returning, and when she finally appeared she was carrying two mugs.

'Hot chocolate.' She put one in Natalie's hand.

'A shade hot for this, isn't it, Mother?'

'It should help you to sleep. I've been working you very hard these past two days, but you're really not eating very much. You look a bit fragile.' Julia had a little worried frown between her brows.

'It's a very loving mother who can describe someone of my proportions as fragile!'

'How you do harp on about your size, Natalie! At times you get downright boring about it.' Julia fixed her daughter with a militant eye. 'Correct me if I'm wrong, but your size doesn't exactly appear in the light of a handicap at the moment. Sam Wyatt sticks to you like glue, poor boy, and when you came bursting in so precipitately tonight I received the impression that Nick might have been making a rather heavy pass at you. If that's what one calls it these days.'

'It'll do.' Natalie scowled into her mug.

'What's the matter, then, love? Or am I being a nosy old woman and behaving too much like the heavy parent?'

'Don't be ridiculous.' Natalie looked pensive. 'In fact Mr Marlowe seems to think I've gone my own way too much and that I neglect you.'

Julia was taken aback.

'Of course you don't! I'll admit I'd like to see a bit more of you, especially now Cordelia lives in France, but I appreciate that your job is very energy and time-consuming. . . .'

'He's right,' interrupted Natalie. 'I think it's time I was more honest. It was Edward who consumed my spare time, and I somehow got out of coming home as much as I should. That's no excuse, Mother, and I'll take care to come down more often in the future. That is one thing the wretched man *is* right about. I'm really quite attached to my undemanding parent, you know.'

'I do know, darling. One doesn't have to be in the same place as a person to love them, after all.'

Natalie got up and gave her mother a brief hug.

'Come on, little Mother, let's go to bed.'

'Not for the moment, Natalie, sit down again.' Julia's voice was unwontedly authoritative, and Natalie obeyed automatically. 'Is Nick being a bit—well, is he rushing you a bit too much?'

'He seems to think he can take up where we left off years ago. I'm not sure I appreciate his rough-riding methods very much. Just because Edward's given me the push there's no reason for me to drop with gratitude into the first pair of arms available, even if the arms have full parental approval. Besides, it's all too sudden. I'm hardly over Edward yet in this short space of time, action-packed though it may have been!'

'Well, darling, you've been trailing round after Nick intermittently since you were five, so it's not really a strange pair of arms, is it?'

'No-o, I suppose not, but there's no reason why he should assume I should be ready to pop into bed with him just because he wants me to, just the same.'

Julia gazed at her daughter aghast.

'Surely that's not his intention, Natalie!'

'Oh yes, it is. He made it crystal clear outside in the garden. I'm not up to that sort of thing, anyway. See-sawing from one man who merely expected the odd chaste embrace to one who wants to take me to bed immediately makes it difficult to adjust.'

'Very good for your self-esteem, though, surely?'

'Possibly. I just wish there was some happy medium between the two.'

Suddenly Julia began to laugh.

'This is hardly a suitable conversation for a mother and daughter!'

'Well, you asked, so I told you.' Natalie smiled unwillingly. 'Anyway, we shall be so busy until Saturday there won't be time for any dalliance of any kind, so let's go to bed. I'll read my lines through before I go to sleep and you can take me through them over breakfast.'

'Right.' Julia got up and turned out the lights. 'Try to have a good sleep. Everything will look different in the morning.'

She was right. When they both arrived downstairs the following day the morning was misty and grey. Julia was flattened.

'All that lovely weather, and now look at it! It looks like being the Village Hall after all. What a shame!'

'Never mind, Mother,' said Natalie soothingly. 'We have a few days yet, the sun will probably return in good time for the play. Now let's get down to Lucy's after breakfast and see if we can get this costume of mine finished.'

From then on Natalie's time was accounted for every second of the day from waking to sleeping and left her no opportunity to miss Nick. Which made it doubly irritating when she managed to do so just the same. Determined not to display this to anyone, not even herself, she threw herself into the preparations so wholeheartedly there was no time for soul-searching, though she avoided Julia's assessing eye whenever possible.

Each time the phone rang in the evening Natalie had to force herself to sit still and let her mother answer it, cursing herself for hoping it would be Nick. Sometimes it seemed life would have been a great deal simpler if she'd stayed put on her own in London to recover from Edward's cavalier treatment. Here at home she was getting over Edward with remarkable success by the simple expedient of risking involvement with Nick all over again. She would sit on the settee late in the evenings with a book on her knee, turning over pages at regular intervals without taking in any of their contents. Every time she remembered Nick's parting words she seethed with resentment. Just because his glamorous existence was over, with all the attendant feminine adulation no longer in abundance, he had no right to think she herself was ready to throw herself into his arms as soon as he beckoned. Perhaps now he considered himself disfigured Natalie Ross was as high as he thought he could aspire, she reflected bitterly. Her guard had slipped disastrously for a moment there in the garden, and Nick had been swift to press his advantage, but to assume from her brief moment of weakness that the battle was over was carrying things too far. At least there had never been any skirmishing like that with Edward. From the first it had been understood that Natalie preferred to keep things on a calm, cool basis, all thoughts of a closer physical relationship to be deferred until they were married. Just as well, she thought gloomily, the way things had turned out.

The problem at hand at this moment in time was trying to keep herself detached and indifferent to the effect Nick had on her physically. At seventeen there had been some excuse for abandoning herself so completely to him. Youth, inexperience and sheer hero-worship had made it inevitable. Natalie gritted her teeth. Surely the intervening years had brought her some measure of maturity and self-control, though if she were completely honest, it was regrettably obvious that any tendancies she might possess towards the physical side of love had never been put to the test by anyone else, not even Edward. She sighed wearily. Odd how one could surprise oneself so completely. Out there in the garden she had wanted Nick with astonishing violence, and had been utterly lost in the shattering surge of feeling his lovemaking had induced. Natalie squirmed. The only course open in the future was to take great care never to be alone with the dangerous Mr Marlowe again.

CHAPTER SEVEN

THURSDAY morning was a little brighter, and Julia's spirits lifted.

'I need some artificial rosebuds,' she said at breakfast, 'Lucy goes into Stratford this morning to deliver some of her pots. We'll beg a lift and treat her to a slap-up lunch, then look for some suitable flowers. I want them for your hair.'

'Good idea.' Natalie was glad of anything to keep herself occupied, and went upstairs to find something a little more respectable to wear than her rather tatty denims. Julia rang Lucy, who appeared at the gate in her little estate car promptly at eleven.

Lucy Armitage had lived in the village all her life, the only daughter of parents now dead, and was one of those people who exuded serenity. Her age was hard to determine; late thirties was Julia's estimate, but a year or two either side could have been just as likely. Her square, strong face was tanned and free of make-up, with wide clear blue eyes serene beneath a fringe of thick fair hair.

Natalie folded herself into the small back seat, looking over at the boxes of pottery in the back of the car with interest. Julia installed herself in the front seat, smiling gratefully at Lucy.

'We're taking you to lunch somewhere nice today, Lucy, as a very small thank-you.'

'That's a pleasant thought.' Lucy started the descent down the hill into the village with care, mindful of her precious load in the back. 'Highly unnecessary, though, a sandwich or something will do.'

'Nonsense! I can't think of any other way to thank you for all the work you've put in on the costumes, especially with your pottery to get on with at the same time.'

'Well, the shop never demands a deadline, though I

95

try to keep production fairly brisk at this time of the year for the height of the tourist season.' Lucy smiled briefly over her shoulder at Natalie. 'Are you happy with Titania's dress, dear?'

'Out of this world, Lucy. It really does give me that ethereal feeling my dear mamma is trying to bludgeon into me.' Natalie hesitated. 'One thing, though, those balloon sleeves—I don't feel they're just right, somehow, to be honest.'

'Funny you should say that,' answered Lucy, 'last night I slashed them from wristband to shoulder, and now they'll just be clasped at your elbows with a garland of flowers, leaving most of your arms bare.'

Julia was delighted.

'That's it! Of course, perfect. My reason for coming in today was to look for rosebuds to dress Natalie's hair, so we'll just get some extra. Do you need anything else, Lucy?'

'As the Elizabethan costumes are coming from the Royal Shakespeare Theatre I've only had to do Oberon, Titania and the fairies.' Lucy chuckled. 'Oberon is hardly wearing anything much at all, so it really hasn't been much of a chore just to dress the fairies and Puck. I've cut quite authentic-looking leaves from felt to scatter over the fairies' tunics, Natalie, sort of a babes in the wood effect, but Puck's is made of a furry material, with one shoulder left bare and an uneven hem, to suggest a Pan-like appearance.'

'Which he more or less has most of the time, even in everyday clothes, so he should look fantastic. My other idea,' went on Julia, warming to her subject, 'was to have all the children make tiny masks out of gold foil, just to cover the eyes as a finishing touch of unreality. What do you think?'

'Don't tell me I have to wear a mask?' Natalie was definitely put off by the idea.

'No, darling, not during the play. I shall make you and Oberon two special masks with handles to hold in front of your eyes for the final dance.'

'What final dance?' asked Natalie in alarm.

'Instead of taking bows, all the characters are going to leap around the stage to Mendelssohn in a mad sort of polka, in pairs. At which point I thought Oberon could wear a cloak of gold-spangled gauze.'

Both Lucy and Natalie collapsed with laughter at this last.

'Poor Sam! Will he ever live it down, I ask myself,' sighed Lucy. 'Only the consolation of having Natalie as Titania is keeping him going!'

After lunch they completed the necessary purchases and arrived back at Arden-under-Hill in time for the evening rehearsal. It went very well, and by Friday evening the performance was even better, with a virtually word-perfect cast, and exits and entries effected slickly with exact timing. The amateur-painted canvas flats blended in surprisingly well with existing greenery, and the sound system worked efficiently, as did the lights.

Sam Wyatt had developed the tendency to stick to Natalie's side like her shadow in Nick's absence, also his final scene of reconciliation with her in the play was rather more ardent than was strictly necessary. There were no actual stage directions in the text, of course, but Julia felt it gave emphasis to the reinstatement of their harmony for Sam to give Natalie a kiss and embrace as their differences were resolved. Natalie had private reservations about the fervour which Sam brought to this particular part of the play, though, to be just, it was hard to fault him on his performance in any other way. His splendid physique and resonant voice gave great authority to the role, and it was discovered as a bonus that his singing voice was equally good; untrained, but powerful and true. It was at the final run-through of this scene, when Sam's usual bone-cracking embrace enveloped Natalie, that she became aware of Nick standing on the terrace, watching them with a grim, brooding expression on his face that caused her to respond to Oberon with more than her usual enthusiasm.

When the mad, final romp of the closing dance was over Nick came down to join them, looking alien and remote in his formal city suit among the casually dressed crowd.

'Nicholas, how nice to see you,' said Julia with a warm smile. 'How was London?'

'Hello, Mrs R., London was hot as Hades. I'm very glad to be home.' He turned to Natalie. 'Hello, Nat, how are you now—better?' He nodded to Sam briefly, the large young man quickly excusing himself to go off to join some of his cronies in the White Lion for a well-deserved beer.

'I feel fine,' said Natalie brightly, smiling a brilliant farewell at Sam. 'We've been very busy, of course, up to our eyes, in fact but at least I think we have something like a performance ready to give. You look very tired.'

Despite her careless attitude, secretly her heart was wrung by his air of exhaustion. He looked weary, his face pale beneath its tan, his scar standing out redly, emphasising his drawn, haggard look.

'I don't think I'm quite up to the big city yet, it's a relief to be back.'

Julia had slipped unobtrusively off to talk with some of the cast, leaving Natalie uneasily alone with Nick.

'Have you missed me, Natalie?' His voice was almost inaudible, his eyes glittering like a cat's in the evening light.

'There hasn't been time,' she said airily, avoiding his penetrating gaze. 'We've been rushing around like dervishes with hardly a moment to spare—I was surprised to see you back so soon.'

Nick's eyelids dropped and he rubbed a hand wearily over his eyes, his mouth set in harsh lines.

'That would seem to put me squarely in my place, I think. I was about to say that I could hardly get home quickly enough, but it seems somewhat inappropriate in the light of your evident lack of interest. Still full of maidenly outrage at my parting shot, I gather.'

Natalie looked back at him expressionlessly, refusing to be drawn.

'I haven't given it a thought. You hardly intend me to take it seriously?'

'Natalie, I meant every word I said. You might as

well open your eyes to the fact. It's Nemesis—there's no way you can escape the inevitable.'

She tore her eyes away from the mesmerising effect of his laser-like stare and shrugged indifferently, ignoring the gathering anger darkening his face.

'I'm afraid I don't agree. I prefer my life a little less complicated. Now, if you'll forgive me I'll collect Mother and head for home. Goodnight.'

Natalie gave him a polite, impersonal little smile and walked slowly away to find Julia, inwardly deeply shaken by the tense little encounter, but determined to hide her disquiet at all costs. Nick stood still for a moment, watching her departing figure in glowering frustration, an angry look in his eyes as he turned away in the direction of the house.

Julia frowned at Natalie as they walked home.

'I presume you were unwelcoming, love?'

'Yes.'

Julia sighed.

'You know, Nick has been very kind, lending us his garden, and now giving a party afterwards. Do you have to be quite so hostile?'

'I feel hostile.' Natalie opened the back door of the cottage with a vicious little wrench. 'Wouldn't you, if someone took it for granted that you slept around?'

Julia bit her lip, then gave way to a grin.

'At my age I'd be either amazed or flattered! Seriously though, are you absolutely sure that is really what Nick meant? It seems so uncharacteristic, somehow.'

'Mother, of course I'm sure. Presumably you don't expect chapter and verse, but I assure you he was remarkably explicit. Now let's drop the subject and have some tea and a sandwich.' Natalie turned away to fill the kettle with an air of finality.

Julia obediently began to talk of something else, but watched with misgivings as her daughter drank two cups of tea in rapid succession, chattering gaily about the play all the time, but leaving her sandwich in a crumbled mess when she announced that she was done in, and kissed her mother goodnight.

Natalie found sleep elusive. The weather had cleared during the afternoon and a glowing sunset had left the low-ceilinged bedroom warm, with an airless atmosphere despite the windows opened wide to the starry night. For some time Natalie tried unsuccessfully to read, but her bedside lamp proved seductive to so many suicidal moths she gave it up and lay in the dark, with only the sheet covering her. For some inexplicable reason she felt strangely ashamed of her offhand behaviour to Nick. She twisted and turned restlessly, trying to shut out the thought of his bleak look when he received her snub, her mind in a turmoil. Considering her main objective in her flight home to Warwickshire had been recovery from Edward's behaviour it could certainly be viewed as a success from one angle, but in another direction entirely she seemed to have amassed herself a quite different little heap of problems.

Natalie heaved herself over on her back to lie staring at the ceiling and gave herself up to some honest soul-searching. If she were to be starkly truthful she might as well admit that it was largely her pride that had taken the biggest knock from Edward's change of heart. Added to this was the total disruption of her carefully constructed plan for the orderly, sensible way of life marriage to him would have meant. Her heart had certainly not broken; to say it had even suffered a dent would be an exaggeration if she were honest. It was the seventeen-year-old Natalie who had known all too bitterly what heartache was all about. Protecting her secret anguish, hugging it to herself, constantly on guard against anyone who might suspect how lacerated her young feelings were by Nick Marlowe's careless refusal of her ingenuous offer of herself, the young Natalie had gradually manufactured a layer of insulation between her inner self and the rest of the world that no one was allowed to detect or penetrate.

After Nick's rebuff Natalie had almost immediately gone off to college, away from her mother and Cordelia, the first helpful step along a natural path of progress to a new personality that firmly repressed any turbulence inclined to linger beneath the surface that almost everyone accepted as her normal self.

Almost in the way of self-defence Natalie had avoided returning home more than absolutely necessary, unwilling to run the risk of meeting Nick again on one hand, the other hazard her mother's well-developed sense of perception where her children were concerned. Once Cordelia had Jean-Luc she was unaware of practically anything else, but Julia would often regard Natalie with a wry, questioning look in her eyes, as though wondering what was happening to her once gay, carefree daughter.

'I've managed very well for years, thought Natalie, sighing, and now it's as though those years have been wiped out. Any immunity I imagined I had against Nick was mythical. He affects me now as much as he ever did. Am I in danger of letting my pride rule my natural instincts, I wonder? Natalie was still pondering her true feelings when sleep finally brought her to a temporary rest from her attempts to sort herself out.

The fates decided to be kind and granted a flawless day for the performance. Both Natalie and Julia were up early and spent a busy morning overseeing the placing of the seating on the tennis court and checking that all the last-minute touches had been made to the stage, until finally there was nothing more to do except actually put on the play.

Despite all the noise and clatter there was no sign of Nick. Natalie noted this with misgivings, her eyes turning constantly towards the house while she helped direct the seating arrangements. Julia was here, there and everywhere, issuing instructions to all the willing helpers, and, feeling she was unlikely to be missed, by midday Natalie could hold out no longer and made her way unobtrusively round the back of the big house to the kitchen.

Mrs Corby and her sister were busily occupied with putting finishing touches to various delicacies intended for the after-show party, but the former quickly left the vol-au-vents she was filling and switched on the percolator as she smiled in welcome.

'You and your mother must be dying for some coffee, Natalie—you know my sister Ethel, of course?'

Natalie smiled warmly at the other woman, complimenting her on the mouthwatering display of various quiches spread out on the table, and sat down, her eyes wide at the selection.

'I am rather dry, Mrs Corby, it's hot work out there this morning, though naturally we're delighted it's so fine. I'll call my mother up in a minute, shall I?'

'Yes, please—perhaps you would take some cans of beer down for the men, if you'd be so kind.'

Natalie rose promptly, accepting the proffered cans, then hesitated.

'Is Nick not around this morning?'

'Still in bed, my dear. Got one of those migraines of his. I'll take him up some more tea in a minute, but he's not had anything to eat yet, he hasn't, poor lad.'

Natalie delivered the beer to the enthusiastic recipients and collected Julia to go up to the house.

'Nick's in bed with a migraine,' Natalie told her, a worried frown on her forehead as they climbed the terrace steps.

'Oh, darling, what a shame,' said Julia anxiously. 'I sincerely hope he'll be all right for tonight.' She broke off as they entered the kitchen. 'Good heavens, Doris, Ethel, what a marvellous spread you're putting on!'

The two sisters were highly gratified with Julia's praise and were only too pleased to press on her any delicacy she would accept to eat with her coffee. Natalie noticed a small tea-tray ready on one of the countertops and made a swift decision.

'I'll take this up to Nick, shall I, Mrs Corby?' She avoided her mother's startled eye. 'Where does he sleep?'

'That would be a help, dear—he's in his old room at the back of the house next to the bathroom. The best bedroom is still being decorated.'

Leaving the three women to a comfortable chat over their coffee, Natalie mounted the stairs with the tray, her heart beating a little faster as she approached what she hoped was the right door on the big, dim landing. She tapped quietly and went into the large old-fashioned room, its heavy damask curtains drawn against the bright noon sunlight. Nick lay on his back, the covers down to his waist, his tanned chest bare, one arm thrown across his eyes, his hair in wild disorder.

'Thanks, Mrs Corby,' he muttered indistinctly, 'I'll drink the tea in a minute, if you'll put the tray alongside the bed.'

Natalie quietly did as she was told, then sat gingerly on the side of the bed, touching the clenched hand lying at his side. His eyes flew open as he removed his shielding hand and stared at her incredulously from pain-filled eyes.

'Natalie?'

'Hello, Nick,' she said nervously, suddenly shy. 'Feeling rotten?'

To her surprise his colourless face took on a faintly warmer tinge and he turned his head away.

'What the hell are you doing here?' he muttered ungraciously.

Natalie took a deep breath, restraining the impulse to remove herself from the room at top speed.

'I'm doing my best to play Good Samaritan, complete with olive branch, if you'll pardon the poetic licence.'

Nick's head turned back on the pillow with infinite care, and he looked at her suspiciously.

'Why? You were hardly at your friendliest last night. Perhaps you don't consider me a possible threat on my bed of pain?'

'There is that,' she admitted, smiling faintly, 'but I did rather a lot of thinking last night. . . .'

'And what conclusion did you reach?' he interrupted swiftly.

'No conclusion, really, I just felt I'd been a bit waspish and possibly a little hasty in my judgment. Mother was somewhat displeased with me, actually, pointing out how good you've been about letting us use the garden for the play, and giving a party after-wards. . . .'

'All of which has absolutely nothing to do with you personally, Natalie, I don't need your gratitude.'

'Don't be so difficult!' snapped Natalie, her good

resolutions fading. 'I came here to do my Pollyanna bit and I seem to be having a signal lack of success.'

There was an awkward little silence while she stared down at her hands and Nick watched her tensely.

'I know what's bothering you, Natalie,' he said softly after a while.

'I don't think you do.'

'I think we got our lines of communication snarled up the night before I went to London. Do you think we can have a shot at unravelling them tomorrow after all the excitement has died down?'

She looked at him consideringly, concealing a swift pang of sympathy at the lines of pain etched on his face.

'I suppose we can try.'

An involuntary grin lit his face, despite his throbbing head.

'Somewhat grudging, Nat, but better than nothing.'

'Right,' she said briskly, getting to her feet. 'How about my pouring out this tea, now I've brought it. Can you bear to sit up?'

Nick raised himself gingerly while Natalie swiftly stacked the pillows behind him, taking great care to avoid contact with his bare skin. He smiled wearily as he accepted the proffered cup.

'If I'd known I was having a visitor I'd have made an effort to be more decent. Hardly the way I'd have chosen to get you into my bedroom!'

'Never fear, I always make sure my men are incapacitated before I venture over the threshold,' she assured him flippantly. 'Now, how are you feeling? Honestly?'

'A bit better, actually. I can see straight now, which is an improvement. Another hour or so and I should be back to normal.' He grimaced. 'I won't disgust you with the other stages I've already passed through.'

Natalie smiled sympathetically.

'It's probably best if you stay here for the rest of the afternoon, then you may be possibly fit enough to watch the performance tonight. It would be a shame if you weren't there—besides, you must see me in my costume. I haven't worn it yet as Lucy keeps on thinking of more finishing touches.'

'Don't worry, nothing would keep me away. After all, I can claim some responsibility for hacking about old Bill's original text, so I must be there to watch the finished version.' Some semblance of his normal colour was beginning to return to Nick's face.

'Stay put as long as you can, then,' advised Natalie.

'Will do, bossy lady. What do you intend doing this afternoon?'

'As little as possible. I'm taking my indefatigable parent home to nail her down somewhere to have a rest. I'm sure she has some sort of internal dynamo that keeps her constantly on the go. If all else fails I'll make sure she sits with me in the garden.'

'Any nerves, Titania?'

Natalie paused in the doorway.

'At this precise moment I'm a bit numb,' she admitted, then smiled at the man in the bed with such warmth he blinked. 'I hope you'll be there tonight, Nick. It wouldn't be the same without you.'

After the door had closed behind Natalie Nick lay motionless, just gazing at it blankly for some considerable time. Eventually he remembered the cup of tea in his hand and put it back on the tray untouched, a faint smile on his face as he slid farther down on the pillows to sleep away the last of the receding pain in his head.

After their lunch Julia consented to lie down on her bed for a while, and Natalie settled herself in the garden with a book to relax and prepare herself for the evening. A lot of activity still appeared to be going on over at Arden House, and late in the afternoon she heard what sounded like a very high-powered car zooming at much too fast a pace up the winding drive, noisily audible through the stillness of the drowsy afternoon. Her curiosity whetted, Natalie got up and strolled through the garden and along the path to the big house, ostensibly to check that everything was under control for the evening. A red Lotus was parked in front of the house, and Natalie was just in time to see emerging from it a slim figure in a yellow halter-necked sundress, blonde hair a wild aureole of expertly-teased disarray as she threw herself at Nick and kissed him lingeringly as he came out to greet her. Natalie halted immediately and turned for flight, but was a fraction too late to escape Nick's eye as he caught sight of her instinctive movement of recoil.

'Natalie!' he called. 'Don't go. Come over here and meet Caroline.'

Reluctantly Natalie approached the pair on the steps, hideously conscious of her faded denims and cotton shirt, her hair slightly wild after her energetic morning. The woman standing with her arm linked possessively through Nick's, a proprietorial smile on her wide scarlet mouth, was older than she looked from a distance. Expert make-up did wonders in conveying an impression of youth on a face not as young as its owner would like.

'Hello, Nat,' said Nick, smiling at her in welcome and taking her arm. 'This is Caroline Markham, one of the editors from my publishers. Caroline, meet Natalie Ross—quite literally the girl next door.'

'How charmingly rustic and quaint,' cooed the other woman, holding out a hand tipped with long scarlet nails. 'Do call me Carly, darling, everyone does.'

Natalie touched the proffered hand unwillingly, her smile as polite and meaningless as the other's.

'How nice to meet you. Have you just driven down from London?'

'Haven't I just! I'm too hot for words, but when Nick told me there were village theatricals in his very garden today I just couldn't resist making a flying visit to watch.' She turned to Nick, raising her large blue eyes confidently to his as she moved closer to him. 'Can you give me a bed for the night, darling?'

'Sorry. Most of the house is in the process of redecoration at the moment, but I'm sure they'll give you a room at the White Lion in the village.' Nick smiled indulgently down at her. 'Just bat your eyelashes at Joe Gifford, the landlord, and I'm sure he'll manage something.'

The wide, flashing smile changed to a pout, Natalie noted with distaste, disappointment evident for a moment before the other woman shrugged philosophically.

'Then you'll have to come with me, angel, and lend weight to my pleas.' The blue eyes were faintly bored as they turned back to Natalie. 'No doubt we'll see you later at the show, Miss Ross?'

'Oh yes, you'll see me all right,' said Natalie carelessly, then shot a barbed little look at Nick. '*So* glad to see you've made such a quick recovery, Nick. See you later. 'Bye.'

Ignoring his frown, she sauntered slowly away with a reasonably creditable air of unconcern, aware that both pairs of eyes were focussed on her back. Once back in her own garden she threw herself down on the lounger in exasperation. It just showed how sympathy could be misplaced. This morning she had warmed to Nick and decided to relax her unyielding attitude towards him. The oddly defenceless look about him as he lay in bed had cut through her armour almost to the point where her instinct has been to cradle his aching head on her breast. She wasn't the only one, judging by this afternoon's unexpected arrival—or *had* she been unexpected? thought Natalie suddenly, stung by the idea. Maybe Nick had a whole harem arriving for all she knew. She lay motionless, scourged by a wave of jealousy so scalding and violent she trembled with the force of it. The way that predatory, scarlet-tipped hand had clutched Nick's bare arm so possessively made Natalie want to scream. She threw herself on her stomach on the grass, her hands running through the wildly tangled mass of hair that seemed to shoot off sparks of electricity in the light of the afternoon sun. Perhaps this Markham woman was the college chum Nick begged a bed with in London, she fumed—no wonder he had dark circles under his eyes when he came home. Migraine was a new name for it!

Well aware that she was being childish and unreasonable, Natalie strove to control the feeling of outrage that her sensible half knew was entirely illogical. Unfortunately her less sensible self insisted on reminding her of all those other women who were always knee-deep around Nick in his racing days, according to the numerous photographs published in the newspapers. She had been searingly jealous then, too, but at least the emotion had always been swiftly repressed, with no personal contact to add fuel to the flame. Now he was here in the flesh. Natalie bit back a moan of anquish at the thoughts the last word conjured up, realising she was lying on the same patch of lawn where he had lain on top of her only a few days before. Until some ray of sanity had restrained her she had responded to Nick's mouth and hands with all the naïve enthusiasm of the inexperienced seventeen-year-old who, at least, had known no better. Natalie shuddered with distaste, then resolutely began to pull herself together. She had a performance to give that night, even if it was only 'village theatricals'! Her eyes kindled. Tonight would come as a surprise to that synthetic blonde, though presumably she could hardly be termed dumb as well, or she would scarcely hold down a job as editor.

The light of battle in her eye, Natalie sprang to her feet and went indoors to have a bath and begin the lengthy process of washing and drying her hair, determined to play the role of Titania to the utmost of any talent she possessed. It should be relatively easy after all, she thought drily, stripping off her clothes while the water ran, I've been successfully putting over a completely edited version of myself to the world at large for years. A mere fairy queen should be child's play. She looked at herself in the mirror before stepping into the scented water and was startled to see a warlike expression on her face more in keeping with Lady Macbeth than Titania. I'll show Miss Carly Markham, she thought fiercely. 'Carly', Ugh!

CHAPTER EIGHT

LUCY and Julia helped dress Natalie in the cottage later that evening before they left for Arden House to see to the rest of the cast.

Left alone in the quiet house, Natalie silently communed with her reflection in the pier-glass. She saw an other-worldly creature, unreal, nebulous and ephemeral in the evening light. Subtle pale make-up concealed the freckles. Darker toning blusher emphasised cheekbones and gave her skin a luminosity heightened by eyes darkly shadowed in the hollows and lit with gleaming gold on the lids and on the highlight under brows darkened and extended to tilt at the outer corners. The red of her mouth had gold in it too, giving it the look of a gold-dusted poppy. Fingernails and toenails were painted with sparkling gold to echo the lights from the beads in the stiff gold bodice cut straight across her breasts, leaving her creamy shoulders bare except for the floating sleeves clasped at wrists and elbows with rosebuds. The diaphanous layers of the skirt floated and fluttered with her every movement and her hair hung loose, curling down over her shoulders unconfined except for a few of the top tresses which were braided into small plaits intertwined with more rosebuds.

'Well-met, Titania,' said Natalie to her barefoot reflection. 'You don't look half bad, all things considered; quite fairylike, in fact, to those who like their fairies tall.' She smiled at herself, momentarily taken aback at the way her eyes gleamed back at her through darkened lashes.

She collected her gilt sandals for the walk through the gardens to Arden House, and wandered slowly along the box-lined gloom of the path, something in her mood already in tune with the atmosphere of enchantment engendered by the scenes of the play. Natalie drifted to a halt, unsurprised as she saw Nick's tall figure coming towards her. She waited silently in the fading light until he stopped abruptly a short distance away and stood staring at her in complete silence, his own appearance arrestingly attractive in black silk shirt and off-white linen slacks.

'Well?' she said at last, very softly, 'will I do?'

He covered the distance between them and picked up her hand, kissing the gilt-tipped fingers with reverence.

'I'd kneel to you, Majesty, if I were dressed more suitably. . . .'

'No necessity for that, Nick,' she interrupted, going on with gentle malice, 'your migraine might overtake you again. What have you done with Miss Markham?'

He frowned, his mouth tightening.

'Back to square one, are we, Nat? My migraine has gone, completely. I was given a very special cure for it this morning—very special. As for Caroline, I haven't "done" anything with her, she's sitting in the audience at this very minute.'

Natalie's eyes glittered at him archly.

'What a practiced charmer you are, Nicholas Marlowe, to be sure!'

His nostrils flared and his long fingers tightened over hers, making her gasp in protest.

'Cut it out, Natalie,' he said harshly. 'I had no idea Caroline was coming. She's a creature of impulse, and I suppose I must have mentioned the play, so she just took it into her head to drive down.'

Natalie gazed up at him innocently.

'There's no need to explain, Nick—it's nothing to do with me, after all.'

With a stifled curse his hands shot out and grasped her bare shoulders, shaking her slightly, rocking her back on her flat heels.

'If it were possible to give you a good spanking without disarranging your finery I'd turn you over my knee right now, Natalie Ross. As it is I'll defer retribution until some more suitable juncture.'

Deliberately Natalie removed his hands from her

shoulders with an air of delicate distaste that only served to enrage him further.

'Damn it, Natalie!' he began explosively, but she turned away and started for the house, chatting politely in a way that obviously set his teeth on edge.

'It's really getting rather late, I think I'd better hurry, Nick, or Mother will be wondering where I am. Did you see the others, are they all ready?'

He took her arm, ignoring her instant recoil, and guided her along a less used path leading round the back of the house.

'Yes. They all look wonderful. Sam in particular looks extremely impressive.'

Natalie giggled in decidedly un-regal manner as they went quietly through the back door into the dark kitchen.

'He refused to rehearse all stripped off yesterday as my dress wasn't ready, said he'd burst on us unarrayed tonight. Do you think we'll make a good pair?'

Nick held her still, a restraining hand on her arm.

'On stage only, Natalie. Don't give him any hopes you have no possibility of fulfilling, I warn you.'

A great bubble of elation and triumph surged up inside Natalie, but her face showed only a mocking look of enquiry as she faced him in the unlit room, the babble in the hall beyond the closed door a background to their hushed voices.

'How do you know I won't fulfil them? I'm a free agent.'

'I'll make damn sure you don't,' he grated. 'And don't try and push me too far, Natalie—I'm no waxwork, like your precious Edward.'

Eyes narrowed and glinting, she glared at him while his hands took hers and drew her slowly towards him, something in the stance of his body leaving her in no doubt as to his feelings. Desire was emanating from him like rays of energy, rendering her momentarily helpless as his arms slid round her waist, then savagely she wrenched herself free, thrusting away his restraining hands as she whirled in a flutter of draperies and threw open the door into the hall. The excited chatter of the assembled cast flooded in, all of them at fever pitch with excitement as Natalie joined them.

Sam Wyatt stood out like a beacon, his splendid body bare except for the leather breechclout, a gilt thong round his forehead, his eyelids glittering gold above blue eyes filled with suppressed anticipation, the promised gilded spear in his hand. He was gesticulating about something as he talked to the Vicar, who was in workmanlike Elizabethan costume as Bottom, when he caught sight of Natalie and stopped mid-sentence with an audible gasp, and there was a general ripple of admiration from everyone present.

'Looks rather nice, doesn't she?' said Julia smugly.

'Rather an uncharacteristic display of understatement, Julia,' said Holmes dryly.

'Nice?' Sam's voice was charged with feeling. 'She looks out of this world!'

There was an outbreak of excited chatter as Julia twinkled up at Nick.

'A very satisfactory reaction, as it was exactly the effect I was trying to achieve. What do you think of her, Nicholas?'

The man beside her watched Natalie as she was swallowed up into a voluble group of fairies all clamouring to be admired, the look on his face clear for all to read for one fleeting moment before the customary shutter came down in his eyes. He smiled crookedly into Julia's enquiring face.

'Oh, I think you know that well enough already, Mrs R.'

Julia nodded, apparently well satisfied, as she went off to marshal her players into readiness. Nick's eyes followed Natalie everywhere she moved, watching her chat to the young lovers, then to the Vicar and the rest of his henchmen, his jaw set as she teased Sam, deliberately casting a saucy look over her bare shoulder at the man watching her. Julia came back to tell Nick he ought to be taking his place out front.

'She's different tonight, Mrs R., in some undefinable way. Dress and make-up apart, she's like something from another planet. I hope she comes back to earth afterwards!'

'Don't worry, Nicholas. My feeling is that Natalie *has* finally come back to us again. She's been living in some other sphere of her own for a very long time, I believe.' With an enigmatic little smile Julia moved away to join Lucy, leaving Nick to reflect on her meaning as he went out to take his seat in the audience.

Afterwards everyone in the audience agreed that the play had never been done more enjoyably even at Stratford; more expertly, possibly, but the beauty of the natural setting seemed to produce a magic that infiltrated the whole performance and inspired the players to new heights of expression never achieved in rehearsal. Nick had seen the play before professionally, but he was captured by the atmosphere of his own condensed version from the moment that Natalie stepped onstage carrying one of the smaller children as the changeling. Everyone present, even those who normally detested Shakespeare and had been dragged along, were enraptured, from the first line to the last madcap romping dance of all the cast round their grassy stage.

Natalie had found some deep reserve inside herself that produced a performance Julia had never managed to wring out of her in rehearsal, and that Sam responded to magnificently. At the party afterwards they both stood together, still in costume, though Sam's long legs were now clad in jeans as they laughingly received the compliments showered on them both from all sides.

Nick brought Caroline Markham across to the tall, glittering pair, the blonde girl fluttering her eyelashes at Sam even as she spared Natalie a careless compliment.

'Darling, I had no idea you were performing when I met you this afternoon. Tell me who made you up—it's an incredible transformation!'

'Amazing, isn't it, what can be done with a layer or two of warpaint,' agreed Natalie, smiling sweetly.

Carly Markham flushed beneath her own elaborate make-up and shot Natalie a look of acute dislike before turning deliberately away to talk to Nick.

'I had no idea village life was so eventful, Nick my sweet. The mystery of your yen for rural immurement is revealed.' Her hand fastened on his arm in the now familiar possessive grasp, the sight of the long nails, now painted wine red to match her low-cut dress, filling Natalie with a sudden urge to detach the offending fingers by force.

Nick merely grinned and began introducing his visitor to everyone, leaving her in the safe, though witty, company of the Vicar while he himself fulfilled his duties as host, seeing that glasses were filled and that the tempting contents of the buffet table were sampled by everyone. Sam Wyatt took advantage of a slight lull to call for silence in a stentorian voice and proposed a toast.

'To Nicholas Marlowe, who not only let us rampage all over his gardens (and don't forget we want plenty of willing assistance to clear it all up tomorrow!), but who is entertaining us all right royally at this smashing party!'

There were cheers from all sides, laughingly acknowledged by their host, who took the opportunity of refilling Natalie's glass as the noise died down a little.

'Well, Queen Mab, how do you feel now it's all over?'

'Relieved, not to mention a bit exhausted. I don't think my cellular structure can remotely resemble my mother's—just look at her whooping it up over there with the Vicar and his lot! Even the sophisticated Carly is eclipsed.' Natalie shook her head in wonder at the small, gesticulating figure of her mother in fond amazement.

'I think you're even more incredible,' said Nick quietly, standing close to her. 'Something about you tonight, Natalie, makes me—uneasy.'

'Uneasy? What on earth do you mean?' She turned up darkly brilliant eyes to his, their expression mocking.

'I can't rid myself of this feeling that you've gone through some change far removed from mere make-up or costume. I sat there tonight, spellbound, just watching you.' Nick paused, his face serious as he looked down searchingly at her. 'Has something happened to you today, Natalie? You cause an odd frisson of sensation down my spine every time I look at you.'

Natalie smiled into her glass of wine.

'The after-effects of your migraine, I imagine. Let's go over and join Mother and the rest of them; I fancy your Miss Markham is getting restive with all these bucolic festivities.'

From then on the party progressed by leaps and bounds, though drooping small fairies were soon collected by their parents and taken home to well-deserved bed, leaving their elders to celebrate at length, apart from the Vicar, who, like Cinderella, was obliged to be home before midnight, though for different reasons. The only flaw in the evening as far as Natalie was concerned was that she was obliged to leave the glamorous Caroline Markham in full possession of the floor when weariness finally overtook both the Ross ladies, and Natalie and Julia took their leave of their host, who bade them goodnight with some reluctance, unable to desert his guests in order to see them home.

CHAPTER NINE

UNABLE to cope without sleep a moment longer, and feeling almost too weary to stagger up the steep stairs to bed, Natalie said goodnight to her equally tired mother, removed her costume and creamed away the last traces of her Titania make-up. Suddenly she was wide awake. She got into bed and for a while was content to lie basking in the reflected glow of the evening, but the sleep which had threatened to over take her a short time before had completely vanished. For what seemed like hour after hour she made herself lie still, trying to court drowsiness, but eventually gave it up and got out of bed to put on her dressing gown, creeping noiselessly down the stairs, hoping to let Julia sleep undisturbed. Instead of making a drink, her first intention, she unlocked the kitchen door and wandered out into the dark garden, breathing in the cool air with relief, enjoying its perfume, a mélange of lilac and roses blending with the aromatic scent from the herb garden. Natalie drifted along the garden path, gazing up at the stars dreamily when she was startled by a movement near the gate and froze, her heart in her mouth. A tall figure moved and came silently towards her.

'It's me, Nick.' His whisper reached her through the darkness as he touched her trembling hand, and with a moan of sheer relief she threw herself against him, burying her head on his shoulder.

'You frightened me to death!' she complained, sagging limply in the arms that closed automatically round her shaking body. 'What on earth are you doing out here at this time of night, anyway, and what have you done with your seductive guest?'

'The last revellers have just departed. Sam was only too pleased to escort Caroline down to the White Lion, and as I wasn't in the mood for sleep I thought I'd take a stroll, though I certainly didn't expect to meet anyone

116

else at this time of night. My feet seemed to come this way of their own accord—would you believe I've been staring up at your window? I've got my plays mixed up; Romeo, not Oberon!'

Natalie chuckled.

'I've always thought he was a complete twit!'

'I thought you might. A case of type-casting, would you say?'

Natalie stayed where she was for a moment, then said hesitantly,

'I actually got up for a drink—would you . . .?'

'Better still,' he interrupted, 'come and have one with me at the house, then we won't disturb your mother.'

Somewhat to her own surprise Natalie nodded her consent and withdrew from his arms, allowing Nick to take her hand as they strolled in silence through the tree lined path to where the house loomed black against the starlit sky, its age more apparent than by day. In the kitchen Nick switched on two bright strip lights and turned to look at Natalie, who flushed a little, as she tightened the belt of her robe around her.

'I'm not really dressed for visiting.'

'I'm not complaining. I was just about to ask you to ignore the post-party chaos in here; I'm afraid I'm leaving it to Mrs Corby in the morning. Now what would you like—though I rather fear there isn't much choice apart from beer or fresh orange juice. Your actors were a thirsty crowd.'

'Orange juice, please.'

Natalie perched on a corner of the big, immaculately scrubbed table which was the sole survivor of the original kitchen, the rest of the fittings a triumph of modern taste and technology. Accepting the tempting frosty glass, she smiled her thanks, noting how drawn his face still looked, the scar standing out angrily beneath the fair hair that flopped untidily over his forehead as he stooped to take out a couple of cans of beer from the fridge.

'Let's take these into the study,' he suggested, helping her down from the table. 'I've just closed the door on the drawing-room and left it until tomorrow.'

Nick crossed the panelled hall to a small room leading off it under the imposing staircase.

'My workshop,' he said, ushering her into a shabby oblong room lined with bookshelves. It was furnished very simply, just a huge desk, a big leather chesterfield settee, and an old wing-backed chair covered in worn rubbed velvet that matched the equally ancient curtains he drew across the windows. The only modern intrusions were a typewriter and a portable television set. Natalie curled up on the settee, taking in her surroundings with keen interest.

'So this is where it all happens; I've never been in here.'

Nick stretched his long body tiredly beside her and half turned, his arm along the back of the settee, to look at her in thoughtful silence, an expression in his eyes she found disquieting. Natalie fidgeted a little restlessly after the silence began to lengthen.

'What's the matter, Nick?'

He looked away and poured one of the cans of beer into a glass tankard, taking a long drink before answering. Without looking at her he said quietly,

'I was sitting in here earlier, imagining you just where you are now, only I didn't have the temerity to picture a dressing gown. I was mentally writing a scene in an imaginary novel where we were happily spending the evening in perfect amity together, just talking, just being together. Only in my imaginary scene, later we went upstairs, still together, where, still in perfect accord, we went to bed and lay in each other's arms all night. I rather tend towards happy endings, as you can gather.'

Instead of offence at his mention of bed, Natalie's reaction surprised herself as much as it did the man looking down morosely into his glass.

'It's rather a lovely scene, Nick. Why is it making you so—so . . .'

'Bloody miserable?' he finished for her. 'Because, by being somewhat previous the other night, I seem to have destroyed any possibility of its becoming fact instead of fiction.'

Natalie finished her drink and put down her glass, turning to him with a look of candour in her dark eyes.

'The thing is, Nicholas, I think we ought to get certain things straight, and then possibly we can go on from there. In a nutshell, for starters I don't sleep around, so much as I—I like you, and I'm willing to admit that physically we seem to be highly compatible, no way am I going to leap into your bed with you—or into anyone else's, for that matter.' Her colour rose, but her eyes remained steadfastly on his.

He stared at her, his face a worse colour than before, his eyes pale and glittering in the soft light from the gooseneck lamp on the desk. His voice sounded almost stifled as he spoke.

'Is that what you thought I meant?'

'What else?'

'I meant the whole thing as a build-up to something quite different, Natalie. The little tale I was telling had a few more details I didn't fill in; like a couple of children sleeping upstairs, a few toys strewn around the hall—in short, marriage.'

Natalie was struck dumb, and her eyelids fluttered downwards. She stared at her clasped hands, noting a ragged nail irrelevantly, afraid to look up into his face.

'I'm stunned,' she said at last, very quietly.

'So I can see,' Nick said wearily, getting up. 'Don't let it disturb you, I realise I'm out of line. Come on, I'll walk you back.'

Natalie stayed where she was.

'Sit down again, Nick, we can't dismiss a statement like that as though it had never been made.'

He obeyed without looking at her.

'You've only known me for little more than a week,' she began.

'Correction—I've known you since you were a little girl.'

'Yes, granted, but seven years have elapsed in between, growing up years for me, plus Edward, hectic years for you with great changes, and goodness knows how many women you've been associated with in that time.'

Some of the deadness faded from Nick's face as he came a little nearer to her, his arm once more along the back of the settee, but taking care not to touch her.

'I've known a lot of women, of course, I'm completely normal, but I assure you that I've never asked one to marry me.'

'I'm not perfectly sure whether you've asked me.' Natalie looked sideways at him doubtfully, a little frown creasing her forehead.

'Aren't you?' His eyes bored into hers. 'I thought I'd made myself crystal clear.'

'I still feel you don't know me sufficiently well; a few days is hardly time enough to make a decision like that.'

'Rot!' he said forcefully. 'One moment I was sloshing paint about with great enjoyment, the next I turned and saw you standing there in very obvious disapproval. That green dress was blowing in the breeze, a scarf tied round your forehead and you were scowling; something of a mixture between a pre-Raphaelite painting and one of those girls Patrick Lichfield photographs for expensive calendars.' He held up a hand to quell her automatic protest. 'My immediate reaction wasn't "That's Natalie Ross come home to mother", but "That's the girl I want, at last, in my bed at night, at my breakfast table in the morning, for ever and ever, amen".'

Natalie was at a loss for words, her eyes dark with disbelief as he moved closer.

'My reaction was nothing like that,' she said, biting her lip, 'I just thought "Oh no, not Nick Marlowe as well!", it all seemed too much at once. I—I find it extraordinarily difficult to credit you really mean all this.'

'I mean it,' he said quietly.

Natalie smiled suddenly into Nick's intent eyes.

'I'm happy you didn't really think I was—well, available.'

'Hardly very complimentary to me, Nat, how could you think I'd treat Julia's daughter like that, apart from my personal feelings towards you. She'd have me drawn and quartered!' The first glimmerings of a smile were at last touching his mouth and beginning to lighten the sombre gleam of his eyes.

Natalie smiled in response, glad to see him looking appreciably better.

'Fat chance. She's been busy pleading your cause, don't you worry.'

'With any success?'

'Not a lot.'

'And now?'

Natalie looked away in confusion.

'Nick . . . I . . . .'

Abruptly he slid to his knees in front of her, and smiling in a way that made her heart begin to behave in an alarmingly acrobatic way, he placed his hand on his heart.

'Miss Ross, it would give me infinite pleasure—and you, I hope—if you would consent to do me the honour of accepting my hand in marriage. Though, to be scrupulously honest,' he added, grinning, 'I feel it only fair to make it clear that the rest of me comes with it.'

Natalie grinned back.

'Idiot! Now I suppose this is where I say "this is so sudden" and have the vapours, whatever they are.'

'Well?' he demanded, serious again.

She took her courage in both hands.

'Please don't be annoyed, or hurt, if I say I'd like to be courted a bit, coaxed and wooed, just like an old-fashioned heroine; firmly convinced, in effect, that you mean everything you say—or am I asking too much?'

Nick rose from his knees and sat down beside her, pulling her out of her corner to sit on his lap, cradling her in his arms with her head on his shoulder.

'Done. But just until you go back to London,' he conceded, smoothing her hair, 'but you don't leave Arden-under-Hill without a ring on your finger. Then you can give in your notice at your job—presumably a month will do—and come home and live with me and be my love—after the necessary visit to St Luke's,' he added hastily, smiling down into her bemused eyes.

'It's all a bit hard to take in, Nick.' Natalie still felt uncertain.

'You need convincing!' His arms tightened round her, his voice deepening as he went on. 'Perhaps the following little tale might add weight to my utter sincerity. All those years ago, Natalie, when you offered yourself up to me so trustingly, the adoration shining out of those beautiful eyes, it took every last atom of willpower I possessed to laugh in your face and turn you down.'

Natalie twisted in his hold to stare up at him, but she relaxed again as he laid a finger on her lips to keep her silent.

'I wanted you all right—my God, how I wanted you!' he went on savagely. 'Every instinct told me to pick you up and rush off with you there and then, to ignore the effect it would have on your family, and all the publicity that would rage round your unsuspecting head. It would have been throwing you to the lions, my love, and the sane side of me realised it only too well and prevailed, so I let you go, in the only way I believed would be effective. It was effective all right, wasn't it? The sick, hurt look on your face has haunted me night and day ever since—your eyes have come between me and any other woman I ever tried to relate to.'

'Why did you never try to see me again?' she asked, stunned by his revelation, only half believing what she was hearing.

'I did, shortly after I left the track, but I found out you were engaged, very much entrenched in the way of life you'd made for yourself. It seemed like my just deserts, as it was exactly what I'd told you to do, so I buried myself in my writing until fate took a hand and I was left this house. You know the rest.'

Natalie slumped in his grasp, unable to accept that all this time had been wasted. While she had been so busy trying to transform herself into someone else, apparently the only thing wrong with the young Natalie as far as Nick had been concerned had been her very youth.

'How stupid can you get?' she exploded, struggling upright, and startling Nick considerably. 'To think that

I've been grieving all these years and making do with someone else, only to find that to some degree you've been doing the same thing, except that your consolations seemed to be supplied by the dozen!' With sudden violence she pushed him away, anger filling her at the sheer folly of the whole situation. She shook off his restraining hands and turned on him like a tigress, eyes flashing, her voice huskier than usual with sheer temper.

'If the only thing stopping you from taking me was youth, Nicholas Marlowe, why in heaven's name did you leave contacting me so long? Time is a wonderful infallible cure for youth that happens to us all—a year or two would have been quite different. Of all the morons——'

Natalie was rudely interrupted as Nick hauled her unceremoniously back into his arms, silencing her in the most effective way possible by bringing his mouth down hard on her open one. He drew back a fraction, whispering against her mouth,

'I love you. I want you. Now. So believe me and shut up and just kiss me!'

As Nick's mouth returned to hers, less violently this time, Natalie gave herself up to his kiss with such ardour that a great shudder ran through him and he tightened his arms round her savagely, tipping her head back with the force of an overwhelming surge of feeling that left them both helpless against its drive. Trembling and helpless, Natalie let him push her down on the settee, welcoming the weight of his long, hard body against hers as he kissed her face in fierce, almost desperate kisses, his hands caressing and stroking her to fever pitch. When he untied her robe, instead of hindering him her hands frantically helped him strip it off and throw it on the floor. Nick's eyes devoured the length of her, half revealed in the brief pink lawn nightdress, their usual grey-green darkened almost to black, with a look in them that half excited, half terrified her.

He pushed the straps of her nightdress from her shoulders, following his fingers with his mouth, caressing, kissing, nibbling, then catching one taut nipple between his teeth. She reared up against him, gasping his name, and he wrapped his arms hard round her, kissing her hair and nuzzling her neck with his mouth until she subsided against him, and surrendered mindlessly to the demand of his lips on hers, her hands stroking restlessly over the silk that covered his shoulders, while his own hands roamed over the pliant curves that surrendered themselves unconditionally to his touch.

'Natalie, Natalie,' Nick gasped eventually, burying his face in her wildly tangled hair, 'I can't—we can't—darling, this is too much, or rather it's not nearly enough. I'm taking you home.'

Natalie's eyes opened slowly, their expression dazed as they looked up into the infinitely tender expression of the eyes that looked down possessively into her flushed, drowsy face.

'I want to stay with you, Nick,' she whispered.

'My angel, the church clock just struck three,' he groaned, almost cracking her ribs in one last embrace, 'what if your mother wakes up and finds you missing?'

Natalie came to earth with a crash.

'Oh lord, Nick,' she exclaimed wildly, searching for her sandals, 'I never thought of that—I must fly!'

Nick wrapped her robe round her, tieing the sash tightly and smoothing back the tangle of hair from her flushed face, unable to resist one last kiss on her mouth that was poppy red from all the previous kisses.

They stole through the garden like guilty children, hand in hand, but to their relief there was no light in the cottage and all was quiet.

'What are you doing tomorrow?' Whispered Nick, holding her close.

'Nothing much—perhaps lie in a bit in the morning.' Natalie pushed herself even nearer to him.

'Oh, darling,' he groaned, 'I don't want to go home at all.'

She stretched on tiptoe to kiss his scar.

'But if I came back with you now it's glaringly obvious what would happen. The sensations you arouse in me, Nick Marlowe, are definitely not decent!'

He swallowed audibly.

'We shall have to avoid that particular set of circumstances for the time being,' he agreed. 'I can take only so much, madam, of your highly inflammatory effect. By the way, do you want to keep it a secret? Shall we be very discreet and pretend we're just good friends?'

He felt Natalie shake against him.

'We'll be lucky if someone doesn't put two and two together, apart from Mother, who will know at a glance!'

'If it were up to me, poppet, I'd rush in and get your mother out of bed right now, possibly make a phone-call to your sister in Paris, then send the town-crier round the village tomorrow, but I suppose you want to keep to your terms.'

'Just a week, my darling,' Natalie whispered into his neck, kissing the instantly taut muscles of his throat.

'Oh,' he said breathlessly, 'I suppose you think you can get whatever you want by doing that. You'd be right, too! Now, bed——'

'How you do go on about bed!' She gave a muffled little chuckle.

Nick slapped her on her rear and pushed her into the house.

'I'll be over for coffee about eleven. Goodnight, love.'

'Goodnight.' Natalie's answer was almost inaudible as his hand released hers reluctantly, and she slipped silently into the house.

CHAPTER TEN

NATALIE'S second attempt at sleep that night met with instant success, and she was out to the world as soon as her head touched the pillow. She slept like the dead until nine, then woke up to instant recall of the events of the night before, which came flooding back in a tide of happiness. She lay basking in the remembered glow of Nick's lovemaking for a while, then sprang up out of bed feeling full of energy and ready to tackle whatever the day had to offer.

The sun was pouring down in full force and Natalie dressed in a pair of brief white tennis shorts and a man's brown and white checked shirt knotted round her middle. She plaited her hair in two thick, undisciplined braids to hang either side of her face and ran barefoot downstairs, humming one of the songs from the play in a shamelessly off-key voice.

Julia looked up from the morning paper, blinking.

'Morning,' said her daughter blithely, 'is there any bacon?'

'Yes, of course.' Julia refrained from comment and handed Natalie a plastic container. 'Eggs?'

'Please; and a tomato? No, don't you bother, I'll do it.'

While her daughter chanted away about 'spotted snakes with double tongues' to the accompaniment of the sizzling frying pan, Julia made a pot of tea and put bread in the toaster.

'Have you had breakfast, Mother?' asked Natalie over her shoulder.

'Well, no, I wasn't very hungry. I've been drinking tea and wrestling with the crossword. I felt slightly anticlimactic after last night.'

'Only natural, I suppose. I'll put in another rasher and an egg.'

'Thank you.' Julia sat, chin in hand, a slightly dazed look on her face.

When Natalie swung round with two laden plates
and put them on the table with a flourish, she giggled at
Julia's obvious struggle to keep silent in the face of her
daughter's sudden rush of high spirits.

'What's come over you this morning, love?' Julia
could stand it no longer. 'Is all this due to the success of
last night?'

'I feel terrific, that's all.' Natalie tucked in to her
plateful with gusto. 'Anyway, you always say pointed
things about eating a proper breakfast, so here we are,
being good little girls. Eat up!'

Julia did as she was bid.

'Orange juice, Natalie?'

'No, thanks, I had some earlier—much earlier.'
Giggling again like the schoolgirl she closely resembled
this morning, Natalie poured out tea.

'Who was the gorgeous blonde Nick had in tow last
night?' Julia was obviously making an effort to sound
casual.

'His editor, would you believe.'

'Lucky old Nicholas!'

'Well, she probably looks a bit different without all
that make-up. After all, look at the difference it made
to me last night.'

'She's at least ten years older than you,' pointed out
Julia. 'You look just as good this morning without any
camouflage at all. She's probably a complete hag by the
bright light of day.'

'Don't be catty, Mother. Now, what must we do
today? Help clear up?'

'I think we should. We can take a walk over to Arden
House later this morning and supervise the removal of
the seats and the equipment, though I hope someone
else provides the muscles.'

Getting up to clear away, Julia eyed her daughter
with interest.

'You look positively blooming. You must have had
an extremely good night.'

'You never said a truer word, Mother dear, I
certainly did! Now I think I'll indulge in a spot of
domesticity until we go. I left my room in a shambles

last night. I'll buzz round with the vacuum cleaner, and clean up the bathroom while I'm at it.'

'Steady on, darling!' Julia was becoming more bemused by the minute. 'Don't tire yourself out.'

'No chance; I'm firing on all cylinders this morning. Any steaks in the freezer?'

'Yes, I think so. Why?'

'I thought we'd ask Nick to dinner. Let's have some of those tiny new potatoes, a salad and the steak, and I'll make a fruit cocktail. How's that?'

'Lovely!'

Natalie heaved the vacuum cleaner out of the broom cupboard and ran upstairs with it, leaving her mother staring blankly into space. From the slightly discordant version of 'Where the Bee Sucks' floating downstairs Julia thanked her lucky stars it was Oberon who had done the singing the previous evening. Titania had very definite problems in carrying a tune!

Nick appeared while Julia was preparing vegetables. Natalie's bubbling good spirits had been so beautiful to behold this morning that her mother couldn't help hoping they were somehow connected with the man who knocked on the door, a wide grin on his face. She welcomed him with a warm smile, noting with amazement that he, too, seemed to have undergone a sea change. The heavy-eyed, strained-looking man of recent days had been replaced by a smiling, tanned version of the carefree boy who used to visit them every summer years before.

'You look a hundred per cent better this morning, Nicholas,' she said, waving him to a chair while she filled the percolator.

'I feel it, Mrs R. I thought my head was about to burst at one stage yesterday morning—no doubt the result of the mad whirl of city life. Thankfully it let up for me to enjoy the show last night. They did you proud, the play was terrific, and Natalie was the best thing in it. By the way, where is she?'

'Rushing round in a frenzy with the vacuum cleaner, for some reason!'

'No,' I'm not.' Natalie stood in the doorway, smiling happily at Nick, who sprang to his feet, smiling back.

There was an odd, charged little silence, then with a choked sound Natalie flew into Nick's arms, which were open wide ready to receive her as he kissed her soundly, oblivious of Julia, who was watching them with her mouth inelegantly open. When they finally broke apart they both howled with laughter at the look on her face.

'Have I missed a day somehow, or have you two seen each other since last night?' she enquired.

Natalie explained, the words tumbling out as Nick sat down and settled her on his lap, an arm close about her waist.

'We sort of met in the garden, half way. Neither of us could sleep, so we went back to Arden House for a drink and—well. . . .'

'And I formally asked her to marry me,' interrupted Nick, hugging his intended bride even closer, 'which intention I rather thought I'd made clear before, but we obviously got our lines crossed.'

Julia hugged them both, her eyes unashamedly wet, and they all three grew fairly emotional for a moment until the percolator gave a particularly virulent hiccup and Natalie bounced up to pour the coffee.

'But be discreet, Mother,' warned Natalie, 'because we're not officially engaged yet, not for a bit.'

'She wants me to court her for a while longer, yet,' said Nick, his eyes dancing. 'She wants to be wooed, she says. So I've given her a week, then my ring goes on the appropriate finger if I have to tie her down to do it!'

Julia looked quizzically from one to the other.

'And how are you going to keep it a secret?'

'We just won't tell anyone,' said Natalie simply.

'Then I'd advise keeping away from each other in public. I don't like to disillusion you, my dears, but it does rather shine out of you both—well. . . .' She trailed away in confusion.

'You mean it's painfully obvious that I have great difficulty in keeping my hands off her,' Nick said helpfully, dodging a well-aimed kick from one of his betrothed's long bare legs.

'I wasn't about to say just that, precisely,' protested

Julia, her cheeks colouring, 'but you generate a sort of electricity between you. I've been in contact with it before, after all.'

'You mean Cordelia and Jean-Luc,' agreed Natalie. 'We put it down to his being French.'

'I think it's just possibly to do with nature rather than nationality,' laughed Nick, then took time to give Natalie a comprehensive head-to-toe examination. 'I'm cradle-snatching this morning, I think—you look about fourteen.'

'Nothing retarded about me, I assure you,' said Natalie saucily, giving him a kiss, then, swiftly changing to solicitude, 'Your head not aching this morning?'

'Not in the slightest. I've discovered a revolutionary new cure for migraine. I won't shock your mother by elucidating.'

'Nicholas Marlowe! I don't want you to get the wrong idea, Mother,' said Natalie hastily, 'there's nothing shocking I'm keeping from you, I assure you.'

'I merely meant the love of a good woman, darling!'

Julia left them sparring happily while she went upstairs to change. Once they were left alone together the banter died away, and Nick held out his arms. Natalie put her own round him and they stood still, closely entwined for a long interval before he raised her chin and kissed her mouth lingeringly.

'Changed your mind?' he whispered into her hair.

'No.'

'Let me buy you a ring tomorrow!'

'No.'

'Please!'

'I want you to be just a—a suitor for a little while longer. I'm not at all keen on the word "fiancée".' Natalie looked up at him hesitantly. 'Would you mind if I didn't have an engagement ring at all? I'm off those, too. Perhaps I could have one of those wide wedding rings with small stones set in it instead.'

'As long as you let me put it on your finger as soon as possible you can have whatever you like. Natalie?' Nick looked down at her, his face serious, a pulse visibly beating in his temple alongside the scar. 'Tell me!'

'Tell you what?' Natalie swallowed, the look in his grey-green eyes making her mouth dry.

'I think you know very well.'

She hesitated, suddenly tongue-tied, and a shadow came down over Nick's face as he moved to release her. She clutched his arms urgently, pulling them back round her waist as she buried her head against his chest.

'It's not easy to say, not because I don't feel it, but—well, it's broad daylight and—it's difficult in cold blood.'

A peremptory hand jerked her face up to his as a familiar light crept into his eyes like a warning signal and she was ruthlessly seized in unmerciful arms that held her like a vice while he kissed her with such intensity her knees began to buckle. He raised his head a hairsbreadth, staring down at her, unsmiling.

'*Now* tell me, Natalie.'

The excuse of cold blood no longer applied. Natalie felt as though her entire body was one great pulse throbbing with the response she felt. Slowly her lids fluttered down and she said in a voice so quiet he had to bend even closer to hear her!

'I love you, Nicholas Marlowe. If you want total confession, I've loved you from the time I was twelve years old, so it would seem to be a habit I'm unable to break—*Nick*!'

Her breath was expelled suddenly as he crushed her to him with an exultant laugh, kissing her breathless, then he let her go as Julia came in.

As she regarded her dazed, flushed daughter with speculation, her expression changed to one of disapproval as her eyes fell to Natalie's long, bare legs.

'Those shorts aren't really very suitable with workmen and helpers around, my girl.'

'No!' agreed Nick. 'Go and cover yourself, woman—please!'

Natalie obediently started for the stairs, then halted.

'By the way, I'd forgotten about your visitor, darling—what have you done with the cuddlesome Carly?' she asked tartly.

Nick grinned, unembarrassed.

'I went down to the pub before coming here and asked for her congratulations. She sent her best to you, but has to fly—a lunch date in town, I gather.'

'What a shame,' said Natalie sweetly. 'We could all have had a lovely celebration lunch together!'

'Put your claws away and get dressed—or shall I come and give you a hand?' He started purposefully towards the stairs.

Routed, Natalie swiftly did as she was bid.

After a busy day passed in helping with the clearing up at Arden House, Nicholas escorted Julia and Natalie to Evensong, to listen to the Vicar performing his more normal function, then afterwards Natalie prepared dinner for them while the protesting Julia was bullied into putting her feet up.

After its auspicious beginning, the following week was a voyage of discovery for Natalie and Nick in bridging the gap of the years spent apart. They roamed round the Cotswolds in Nick's car, stopping in places that took their fancy, wandering round Moreton-in-Marsh, the Slaughters, the rather more commercialised charm of Broadway and the ageless beauty of Chipping Campden. They talked and talked and grew to know each other all over again, tacitly avoiding any supercharged emotional encounters, letting their mutual exploration proceed at a pace that allowed them to reveal all the facets of their natures to each other, to their shared delight.

Their common interest in antiquities led them to Warwick Castle and on the tourist route of Stratford, from the home of Mary Arden, Shakespeare's mother, in Wilmcote, to the Birthplace in Henley Street. They mingled happily with all the foreign languages and clicking cameras, secure in their own personal cocoon of rapport. At one of the many souvenir shops lining the streets of Stratford Nick paid an exorbitant price for a piece of pottery depicting several hippopotamuses crowding into a dustbin, just because it rendered Natalie helpless with laughter just to look at it. She cradled it to her as if it were a parure of diamonds, and threatened to give it pride of place in the rather faded splendour of the Arden House drawing room.

Every second spent apart was a second wasted, and they clung to their moments together as though they could influence time and postpone indefinitely the end of the week and Natalie's departure. As though the weather realised their holiday was at an end, Sunday was a grey overcast day that reflected their sombre mood, and late in the evening Nick held Natalie close before parting with her. They were standing at the gate in the garden as the church clock struck eleven, in sharp reminder that their time together was over for a while.

'Must you go?' groaned Nick into her hair as he held her hard against him.

'Darling, you know very well I don't want to, but I must. I can't just walk out on my boss; I must give him time to find someone else.' Natalie sighed regretfully, a lump in her throat as tears threatened. Then she laughed shakily up at him. 'After all, I'm not exactly going to Timbuctoo, and I'll be home again next weekend.'

'What time will you get here on Friday evening?'

'As soon as I can possibly make it, but don't expect me before nine, in case the traffic's heavy.'

He rubbed his face roughly against hers, then kissed her quivering mouth, muttering against it huskily,

'For Pete's sake drive carefully, and ring me as soon as you get there in the morning.'

'Yes, darling—oh, Nick. . . .' Her breath left her abruptly as he crushed her to him, kissing her endlessly until she clung to him, trembling, her legs barely able to support her. With a sob she finally tore herself away and fled into the house, thankful that her mother had already gone to bed so that she could indulge in her tears undisturbed.

The following week was an uphill slog all the way. Natalie's boss was dismayed at what he termed her 'desertion', but one advantage of the added chore of advertising for the applicants for her job meant that it added to her usual hectic workload, and made the time pass more quickly. Natalie rang Nick every evening, but otherwise she was extremely lonely, as Maggie Ryan had gone home to Ireland on her annual holiday.

The evenings and nights were the worst part. After each telephone call to Nick the flat seemed lonelier and quieter than ever, and she wandered round it aimlessly, unable to settle to read, or to watch television, or even to gain solace from her usual source of comfort, her opera records. It was increasingly obvious to Natalie that without Nick her life seemed to have no point or direction, and her entire mind and body seemed to be suspended in a limbo-like state until she could be with him again. She knew only too well that none of the feelings was new. She had been through it all before, and had managed to push them away into some far recess of her mind behind a locked door. They had remained there, dormant and in abeyance admittedly, but needing only the slightest relaxation of her will for the door to burst open and flood her being with emotions that had for so long been penned and dammed up. It had only needed one meeting with Nick in person for all the repressed fire to flame into glowing life again, melting the cool outer shell she had grown around herself until now it hardly seemed possible it had ever existed.

Natalie was profoundly thankful when Friday arrived. Her employer was away for the day and she was able to leave the office early, arriving back at the flat by five. She threw some clothes in a suitcase, then removed her office clothes and spent a few reviving minutes in the shower. As she was towelling herself dry the doorbell rang, much to her vexation, hoping it was no one who would delay her in getting away to Nick for a moment longer than necessary. Pulling on her dressing gown, she belted it tightly as she crossed to the door swiftly in response to another prolonged peremptory ring, followed by hammering on the door. Frowning in annoyance, she called out,

'Who is it? Please stop making such a noise!'

'It's Edward. Please let me in, Natalie!'

Natalie stood stock still in surprise for a moment, then shot back the bolt and opened the door in exasperation to the last person in the world she wanted to see at that moment.

Edward brushed past her, pulling her into the room with him, his normally immaculate hair ruffled and his eyes bloodshot, his whole appearance curiously untidy, in painful contrast to his normal demeanour.

'Thank goodness you were here,' he said, his voice slurred and indistinct, and to her intense indignation he seized Natalie in his arms, fastening his mouth on hers before she had time to protest.

'Edward!' She shoved him away in revulsion, retreating a safe distance, glaring. 'What on earth do you imagine you're doing!'

Edward just stood there, swaying slightly, to Natalie's disgust, gazing at her mournfully, and she realised with distaste that he was drunk, almost unrecognisable as the fastidious man of only a couple of weeks before.

'Natalie, I've come back,' he announced dramatically after a pause, lunging for her again.

'Well, I don't want you back!' She sidestepped neatly and he stumbled, collapsing in disbelief on the sofa, his dishevelled head in his hands.

'Give me a drink, please, Natalie,' he muttered indistinctly.

'Certainly not,' she snapped, 'you seem to have drunk more than enough already, by the look of you. Anyway, what exactly are you doing here? Aren't you supposed to be about to trot up the aisle?'

She stood over him, arms folded, amazed to think that she could ever have considered for a moment marrying the man who sat, slumped, his shoulders bowed in abject dejection. Edward looked up at her in misery.

'Lisa threw me over, Natalie. She met someone else—older, with a great deal more to offer, the little flirt. The wedding's off.'

With a sudden lurch Edward heaved himself to his feet, his eyes filled with an unmistakeable purpose, and grasped Natalie by the elbows, rocking her on her heels. She recoiled from the alcohol fumes he exuded, but his grasp tightened.

'Should never have left you, Natalie.' Even his usual impeccable accents were blurred and thickened. 'Good little Natalie, you wouldn't have left me for another chap, would you? A bit too good, that's your trouble—too prim and proper. Should have given me more——'

'That's enough!' Natalie wrenched herself free, eyes blazing with distaste. 'Please go, Edward. I'm sorry you've been discarded for a better prize; not a very pleasant experience, is it? But I'm afraid you'll have to recover as best you can, you're no longer anything at all to do with me. Now, I'm on the point of leaving for the weekend, so goodbye.'

She marched to the door and held it open, waiting pointedly for him to depart. Edward stood unsteadily, looking at her with blank incomprehension.

'But I've come back, Natalie!' He fumbled awkwardly in his pocket for a moment. 'Look, here's your ring. Let me put it on your finger again and everything will be just the same as before.'

Despite her anger Natalie felt a strong tendency to laugh at the utter crass conceit of the man.

'Sorry, Edward, nothing doing. Now please go, or I shall be late.' She held the door wider and stood pointedly waiting, her foot tapping.

In his present alcoholic state Edward was obviously incapable of grasping the fact that she no longer found his presence either desirable or welcome.

'But, Natalie, you don't understand. . . .'

'It's you who doesn't understand, Edward. To be blunt, I had hoped never to set eyes on you ever again. This little encounter has done nothing to change my mind.'

An ugly look came over his sharply cut features, and before she had time to realise his intent he made a swoop towards her and grabbed her to him, picking her up precariously in his arms.

'Edward!' she screamed wildly, struggling in vain while he staggered unwaveringly to the sofa and deposited her on it full length with such a thump that she lay still for a moment, giving him just enough time to throw himself on top of her and force his mouth on hers, which had just opened to emit another shriek of protest.

Her violent struggles only served to inflame him even further, as well as disarranging her dressing gown to the point of indecency. Natalie could hardly believe this was happening. Wildly she fought to free herself, but the normally languid Edward seemed to be invested with some kind of bestial strength that was impervious to her opposition, holding her still with hands that clutched eagerly onto her arms.

Natalie's eyes opened wide in anger and then froze, locked in the icy, grey-green gaze of the man who stood in the open doorway like a figure hewn from stone. Something in her instant stillness seemed to communicate itself to her would-be ravisher as he raised his head to follow the direction of her agonised stare. Edward heaved himself up awkwardly in embarrassment, still unsteady on his feet, but before Natalie could cover herself sufficiently to follow suit Nicholas Marlowe apologised in a voice that transfixed Natalie like an ice-cold dart.

'Do forgive me. The door was wide open, and I had no warning that my intrusion would be so extremely—untimely.'

'Nick! Please!'

Natalie struggled to her feet in despair while Edward stared, stupefied, from one to the other. Before she could reach him, however, Nick gave an odd, formal little bow and left abruptly, closing the door very deliberately in her face. Natalie wrenched it open and ran out on to the landing, but the tall figure was almost at the bottom of the stairs, deaf to her imploring cry, and dressed as she was she was in no condition to give chase, listening to the bang as the outer door closed as though it were her death knell. She turned on Edward in such a raging fury that he physically recoiled before her.

'Get out!' she spat, her face chalk white and her eyes like twin laser beams that pierced his alcoholic haze of self-pity and restored him almost instantly to something like total sobriety.

'I say, I'm sorry, Natalie,' he began haltingly, thrusting his hands through his hair. 'I don't know what possessed me——'

'I'm not interested, Edward. Just go—now!' Natalie's voice had all the salutary effect of a cold sponge on his befuddled sensibilities and he prepared to obey. He stopped for a moment in the doorway.

'Who was that, Natalie?' he asked, straightening his tie and tugging ineffectively at his collar.

'Until your untimely visit he was the man I hoped to marry,' said Natalie stonily, 'so as you have now done as much damage as you could possibly expect to effect in one evening, at the risk of repeating myself, Edward, get out!'

Her voice finally cracked on the last and Edward hurriedly made his departure, still muttering incoherent apologies, even as she shut the door behind him with a crash.

Natalie stood in the middle of the room, her hands pressed to cheeks that burned, despite their pallor. She tried to imagine where Nick might have gone, what he would do now, and what on earth had he been doing here at all when she had been on the point of leaving for home just to be with him. A great tearing sob shook her, but she rigidly controlled the almost overpowering desire to give way to her grief and made herself dress rapidly and make up the colourless face that stared blankly back at her from the mirror with hopeless eyes. Almost beside herself with anguish, she shut up the flat and ran down to her car. The best thing—the only thing—she could do was to go home and hope that Nick was on his way by train so that she could see him later to explain the ugly, ludicrous scene he had interrupted and misinterpreted.

If only the whole thing weren't so tragic it had the elements of pure farce, she thought bitterly as she started the car. A freeze-shot of the little tableau where all three participants were immobilised by shock could have made a splendid poster for a typical Feydeau romp. The expression on Nick's face as he stood there was something she would never erase from her mind if she lived to be a hundred.

The journey home was a congested, protracted
nightmare during which her mind went round in circles
like a rat in a cage. Natalie tried to concentrate solely
on the road after she realised she was passing through
Woodstock with no recollection at all of having
bypassed Oxford. She gathered herself together and
drove the rest of the way with more attention to the
route, but was never more glad in her life to reach
Arden-under-Hill and the comparative sanctuary of Hill
Cottage.

As Natalie parked the car her mother's small figure
appeared in the open doorway, her hands held out in
welcome as the weary girl almost collapsed into her
arms.

Julia held Natalie away from her in alarm.

'Darling, what is it? Are you ill? You look ghastly!'

She drew her daughter into the living room and sat
down on the settee with her, holding Natalie's cold
hands while the girl poured out the sorry little tale.

'It was all so stupid and sordid, Mother, like a scene
out of some second-rate farce. But Nick just left. He
practically slammed the door in my face and gave me
no chance at all to explain!'

Natalie sat, endlessly wringing her hands, her face
full of despair. Julia sighed.

'Men are not likely to be reasonable under those sort
of circumstances, Natalie. Put yourself in Nick's place.
If you'd walked in on him with another woman in a
similar position, half naked as you say you were, do
you think it likely you would have stayed for a logical
discussion?'

'No, I suppose not.' Natalie admitted bleakly. 'I
could murder Edward Herrick cheerfully; the utter
nerve of his behaviour is hard to credit! He never
wanted to do that sort of thing when we were engaged,
yet he had to choose that precise moment to barge in
practically stoned to the eyebrows and go ape for the
first time since I've known him.' She stopped suddenly,
frowning. 'What on earth was Nick doing in London
anyway, Mother?'

'He had the brilliant idea of going up on the train just

so that he could drive home with you.' Julia bit her lip, her eyes full of compassion. 'He wanted to surprise you.'

Natalie laughed hysterically.

'He succeeded beyond all expectations, didn't he?' She rubbed her eyes wearily. 'What do you think he'll *do*, Mother?'

'Come back by train, I expect,' said Julia practically, 'and then you can see him tomorrow and sort things out.'

'But I must see him tonight!' Natalie sprang to her feet, frantic with anxiety. 'I can't sleep with this hanging over me!'

Julia vetoed this immediately.

'I think it would be much better if you both slept on it. It won't look so bad to either of you in the morning. You can go over to Arden House after breakfast—Mrs Corby doesn't go in normally on Saturdays. Now come and have something to eat, you look shattered.'

Full of misgivings Natalie followed Julia's advice and went to bed early, but not to sleep. The sickening, tawdry little scene with Edward re-enacted itself in unceasing repetition in her over-active mind, the look in Nick's eyes as he stood in the doorway etched ineradicably behind her closed eyelids.

As soon as she woke next morning the cold weight on her mind returned in full force, making her almost sick as she bathed and dressed hurriedly before joining her mother in the kitchen. It was a gloomy, overcast day with the threat of thunder, totally in keeping with Natalie's mood, and no amount of persuasion from Julia was able to make her swallow more than a cup of tea. By sheer will-power she remained in the cottage until half way through the morning, trying to read, trying to chat with her mother, trying not to prowl around the house like a caged tigress, and failing miserably in all three. Finally Julia could bear it no longer and pushed Natalie out of the house.

'Go and make your peace, darling,' she said firmly, 'then bring Nick home to lunch.'

Julia was drinking her fifth cup of coffee of the

morning when Natalie returned, disconsolate, ten minutes later, subsiding at the kitchen table, her chin on her hands.

'There was no answer.'

Julia quickly put a mug of coffee in front of her.

'Drink that, love. I expect he stayed the night with that friend of his and he'll travel down today.'

Natalie nodded apathetically and obediently drank her coffee.

The day dragged by interminably. Natalie helped her mother with some gardening after lunch, pushing the lawnmower with a ferocity that did nothing at all to relieve her frustration and anxiety. She clipped and weeded and tidied with concentration, even managing to chat spasmodically to Julia, who wisely let her work as hard as she wanted in an effort to pass the time. Eventually there was nothing more Natalie could think of to do, and the two women went indoors to change. At seven Natalie surrendered to the fierce urge to seek Nick out.

'I think I'll just take a walk over to the house, Mother,' she said, a tremor in her husky voice, 'surely he's back by now.'

Julia watched her go in trepidation.

Natalie's feet began to drag as she drew close to Arden House, apprehension clutching her with a cold hand despite the oppressive evening. A distant rumble of thunder sounded as she reached the heavy front door, which now stood open to what little air was available.

'Nick?' she called tentatively, reluctant to walk in as she normally did.

When his tall figure appeared from the kitchen her heart lurched to her throat, threatening to choke her. In the dim light of the dark panelled hall it was impossible to see his face, though something in the way he stood unmoving chilled her to the bone. His black shirt and cords added to the air of implacability he wore like a shield.

'Come in, Natalie.' He led her into the refurbished drawing-room and waved her politely to one of the

faded brocade sofas. Natalie's heart now reversed itself
and sank to her toes. They looked at each other in
silence, Nick's face expressionless as he leaned against
the white marble mantelpiece, his eyes cold beneath the
angry scar, and she realised sickly that he was not going
to be the one to break the lengthening silence. She
swallowed with difficulty. This was proving more
hideous even than anticipated.

'When did you get home?' she asked finally, her voice
almost unrecognisable.

'Last night. Late.'

Natalie raised wounded, hopeless eyes to his.

'Last night? Why haven't you been over?'

'I didn't see much point.' He sounded slightly bored.

A great pain was beginning to flower inside Natalie's
chest, expanding and flowing through every part of her,
making it almost impossible to breathe.

'It wasn't the way it looked, Nicholas,' she said
quietly. 'Edward was drunk. I'd never seen him like that
before.'

Nick made a violent, irritable gesture of negation.

'Please, don't trouble to go on. He came back, I
presume, and you welcomed him with open arms. From
the brief illuminating glimpse I had you were
welcoming him with considerably more than that.'

'It was nothing like that, Nick. Please let me
explain—it was all a mistake. . . .'

'On all sides,' he thrust in coldly. 'I was a fool to
think you'd get over him so quickly. I shan't make the
same mistake twice.'

A great flash of lightning suddenly streaked through
the room and thunder cracked overhead almost
simultaneously. Natalie barely noticed, so immersed in
her humiliation and grief that she was numb to
everything else. She rose to her feet with infinite care, as
though the weight of years was on her, and looked up
at him from eyes like dull, dark pools in the pallor of
her face.

'You refuse to listen to the truth, then, Nicholas?' she
said quietly.

'It was all only too self-evident, my dear.' He thrust a

hand through his hair and turned away, shoulders hunched as he stared down into the empty fireplace, refusing to look at her. 'I regret I have no aptitude for sharing.'

Natalie winced, then straightened her back.

'Goodbye, Nick.' She turned towards the door, every last shred of willpower she possessed hiding the dull agony that was eating her up inside.

He turned and waved a negligent hand towards the window.

'You can't go out in this weather. Wait until the storm passes over, otherwise you'll be drenched.'

She shook her head.

'What does that matter?'

Unhurriedly she went out into the garden, ignoring the torrents of rain that soaked her instantly, plastering her hair to her head and shoulders and moulding her green dress to her body like a second skin.

The man watching her sombrely moved instinctively to follow, then checked himself sharply. The image of the tableau he had interrupted rose vivid and unforgettable, to the point where his anger erupted in him again with the bitterness of bile, and he smashed his fist in impotent rage and pain into the solid oak door that he closed with a bang to shut out his view of the slowly receding figure of the girl as she trudged along through the downpour.

Blind and deaf to the storm raging around her, aware only of the misery within, Natalie thought detachedly that this was what it must be like to die. All the feeling in her mind and body seemed to be draining away, leaving her numb against the rain emptying down. Even the thunder seemed like gunfire in some distant battle, rather than a storm raging overhead. Her pace slowed a little as lightning flickered in her face. Normally she would have raced for home like a startled deer, but today nothing mattered but the sick feeling of rejection and loss that poured over her in an icy flood, deadening her senses to all other reactions. How naïve she'd been! Despite her nervousness and misery about seeing Nick again she had never for an instant considered the possibility that he would refuse to listen to her. Natalie shuddered as she reached the garden gate. The look of chill disinterest on his face was something she'd never be able to forget. Overcome by cold, sick despair, as she went indoors Natalie began to shiver uncontrollably, shock waves rippling through her as her mother came swiftly into the kitchen.

The latter took one look and said nothing at all, merely putting an arm around the drenched, white-faced girl and leading her up to the bathroom, where she ran hot water into the bath and then stripped Natalie's clothes off without ceremony. Natalie lay docilely in the bath while Julia rubbed her hair with a towel, submitting dumbly to all her mother's ministrations and allowing herself to be put to bed as if she were a child again. Neither spoke a word apart from the soft sounds of comfort Julia uttered as she tucked Natalie in, then she went downstairs to make a hot drink. Natalie accepted the mug and drank deeply, then spoke for the first time. Julia had put a generous dollop of brandy into plain hot milk, and its effect was almost immediate on the overwrought girl.

'I'll go back to London tomorrow, Mother.'

Julia stood looking down at her in silent compassion. 'Nicholas wouldn't accept any explanation, I gather?'

'No. I tried, but he refused to listen. So I'll go back and withdraw my notice at the office—Mr Whittaker will be pleased, at least. He disliked all the applicants for the job.' Natalie smiled valiantly. 'I was thinking, Mother. Under the circumstances you'll forgive me if I don't come home for a while, but there's no reason why you shouldn't come and spend a weekend with me now and again. We could go to Kew and Hampton Court, and do all those things we've never had time for. You can have my bed, and I'll sleep on the settee.'

Julia would have agreed to go into orbit round the moon if it would help take away the dead look from her daughter's eyes.

'Fine. Good idea, I'll look forward to it.' She had difficulty in keeping her voice steady. 'As long as we don't run into Edward Herrick—I'd probably be arrested for a breach of the peace! Perhaps we might pop off to Paris and spend a weekend with Cordelia some time soon, too.'

Natalie nodded, smiling resolutely, then slid farther down into the bed while Julia took herself off, mentally consigning both men to the devil.

CHAPTER ELEVEN

NATALIE drove back to Chiswick on Sunday evening, her heart heavy. Providentially the traffic was fairly light, as her powers of concentration, like her spirits, were at a very low ebb, and, try as she might, there seemed no way of banishing Nick's face from her mind, its expression grim and hostile, yet at the same time wounded. If only he would have just listened, she thought hopelessly, a thought suddenly striking her with mirthless humour. Only a short while ago he had actually said there was very little he wouldn't forgive her, yet she had hit on the unforgivable exception without even trying.

Hoping Maggie might be home from her holiday by this time, when she reached Chiswick Natalie found an open off-licence and bought a bottle of wine, recklessly adding a bottle of vodka on impulse. If men would keep jilting her with such monotonous regularity surely she was entitled to indulge in something to help anaesthetise the shock, she thought, with a sad little smile. To her disappointment the flat was quiet and empty when she let herself in, so Maggie was either out, or still en route from Ireland. Natalie first made a brief telephone call to her mother, then methodically unpacked, fiercely quelling the salty scald of tears as she put the swirling violet dress on a hanger.

The television offered nothing to interest her, so she poured herself a generous vodka and tonic and fell back on her usual standby of music, putting her favourite Verdi on the turntable. This time she chose *Othello*, smiling wryly at its suitability, and settled down to listen to Placido Domingo in his splendid version of the jealous Moor. At least Nick stopped short of actually murdering me, she reflected, though if looks could have killed both Edward and I would have perished on the spot! Eventually a second drink to accompany the music helped even more, blurring the sharp edges of her grief and softening the harsh prospect of setting about recovery from her abortive devotion to Mr Nicholas Marlowe yet again. You'd think you'd have learned by now, she sneered at herself, in fact you should be quite expert at picking up the pieces and glueing them together. You've done it before—no doubt you can manage it again.

When the phone rang a little later Natalie was only the very slightest bit unsteady on her feet as she jumped up to answer it, though her legs were a little disobedient, giving her a curiously disembodied feeling.

'Darlin',' said Maggie's lilting voice cautiously. 'Is it all right if I come home? I'm just off the train, but if you have company I'll go straight to bed with a mere dignified nod in passing, I promise.'

'No problem,' said Natalie airily, 'you'll be more than welcome; there's nobody here apart from Giu— Giuseppe.'

'Is that a fact? Whatever happened to what's-his-name, and who the dickens is Giuseppe?' Maggie was plainly taken aback.

'What's-his-name has given me the push, and now Nick has just done the same—oh, and Giuseppe Verdi composed O-Otello,' Natalie said with due care. 'Sorry; I've just had a comforting little drink. Well, two comforting little drinks, actually.'

'Have you now! Don't have any more, I'll be there in a jiffy. I'm just round the corner in Guido's coffee-bar.'

'These Italians are everywhere!' giggled Natalie.

'Holy Mother!' With a pious retort the other girl put the phone down.

Maggie erupted into the flat ten minutes later, panting with the exertion of lugging two suitcases up the stairs.

'I'd have been quicker, but one of the housemen from the hospital was in Guido's and I had trouble getting away from him.'

'Strange,' said Natalie, smiling cheerfully at her, 'the men I know all seem to want to get away from me.'

'I see.' After one searching look at Natalie's face Maggie made purposefully for the kitchen to put the kettle on, followed more indolently by Natalie, who draped herself against the kitchen door and watched idly while Maggie made coffee and ham sandwiches from provisions supplied by Julia.

'Now then, Natalie Ross,' Maggie demanded, picking up the laden tray, 'what in the name of the saints has been going on while I've turned me back, and who the devil is Nick?'

Natalie obediently ate sandwiches and drank black coffee, pouring out the whole sorry tale to her riveted listener, who munched hungrily in complete silence except for the odd colourful exclamation here and there while she heard Natalie out, varied expressions of anger, amusement and sympathy chasing across her vivid features as the saga unfolded.

At the end of it Natalie felt drained, but surprisingly better, not to mention sober, as though talking about her grief had eased some of the pain while the black coffee did the rest. She was able to help Maggie wash up with a reasonably clear head, though the other girl firmly put away the wine and vodka, a disapproving look in her eye.

'No more of that, Natalie Ross. Goodness sakes, to think you let me go away without telling me about Edward!' She turned a sparkling blue eye on her companion. 'Though as well you know, it's good riddance to that one as far as I'm concerned, and as for this Nicholas Marlowe, don't worry, darlin', he'll come round when he's had time to simmer down. Don't be upsetting yourself any more.'

Maggie's irresistible common sense had its usual effect on Natalie, and she went to bed that night determined to agonise no more over Nick, Edward, or any other man likely to offer any possible threat to her peace of mind. To perdition with them all, was her final thought before falling asleep.

Next day at the office her boss, Charles Whittaker, received Natalie's news with blatant enthusiasm, hardly bothering to express his regrets at her change of plan in his pleasure that she was staying. Somebody wants me, at least, she thought sardonically, as she rattled through polite letters of regret to all the applicants for her job. After that the usual Monday maelstrom of work caught her up and she was too busy to have time to dwell very much on her troubles. The telephone on her desk rang for the umpteenth time at midday, and she picked it up absently as she checked a report for errors.

'Mr Whittaker's office,' she said mechanically.

'A private call for you, Natalie,' said the girl at the switchboard, 'a Mr Marlowe. Can you take it?'

Natalie's heart did a somersault, she was silent for an appreciable moment, then her eyes hardened.

'Tell him—just tell him I'm busy, Carol,' she said finally.

'Will do.' The girl rang off and Natalie put the telephone back on the cradle with infinite care, taking a deep breath and mentally applauding her own strength of will. She returned to the report in hand with determination.

During the afternoon Nick rang twice more, but Natalie gave the same answer, finally telling Carol at the switchboard that as far as Mr Marlowe was concerned she was indefinitely unavailable. After working fairly late that evening she arrived home to find Maggie there before her, preparing the evening meal and bursting to tell her that Nicholas had rung.

'What did I tell you, darlin'?' cried Maggie jubilantly.

Natalie sat down calmly to her meal, to the other's surprise.

'He's rung the office at intervals all day, but I refused to speak to him.' Her mouth tightened bitterly, to Maggie's dismay. 'And should he ring again this evening, Maggie, I'd be glad if you'd just tell him I don't want to speak to him.'

'Ah, Natalie, are you sure that's what you want?'

'Yes, perfectly sure. On reflection, I find condemnation for something I didn't do hard to forgive. It's injustice. I honestly don't feel like talking to Nick—if I do I may say something totally regrettable, so I'll just avoid the whole issue. These chops are delicious, by the way.'

Recognising a change of subject when she heard it, Maggie surrendered to the inevitable and started to talk of her first day back on Men's Surgical. When Nick did ring a little later, despite an agonised look of appeal at Natalie, Maggie obediently relayed the curt little message and finally put the phone down sadly.

'I don't know what he looks like, darlin', but he has the sexiest voice I ever heard,' she said. 'Are you sure you want to keep to this; he sounds absolutely wretched, the poor man.'

A wave of pain washed over Natalie. She almost wavered for a moment, then back flooded the memory of the scene on Saturday, when her vain pleading for a hearing had met with stony refusal, and her resolution strengthened.

'I'm sure. If he rings again when you're here, you can give the same answer, Maggie.'

'And what if he rings when you're alone?'

'Simple. I shall just put the phone down. As you say, it's not the type of voice one doesn't recognise instantly.'

Maggie sighed, obviously disapproving, but aware that for the moment Natalie was immovable. She was solidly behind Natalie a few evenings later, however, when, to Natalie's outrage and surprise, Edward presented himself at the flat, an offering of flowers in hand. Natalie looked him up and down in contempt, taking inordinate pleasure in the colour that suffused his shocked face as she shut the door in his face, flicking her hands together afterwards as though ridding herself of something distasteful.

Maggie watched her with awe.

'Aren't you the fierce one these days! Fancy that popinjay daring to show his nose here. Let me answer the door next time, love!' she begged.

'By all means.' Natalie smiled quizzically. 'I somehow don't think he'll repeat the episode, though.'

She was wrong. The following week Edward tried again, and this time Natalie shut herself in the kitchen while Maggie took a disgraceful amount of pleasure in telling him at considerable length that he and his flowers were persona non grata, and would he kindly find some other door to darken. Edward's affront was so great at Maggie's tirade that he took what could hardly be described as the hint, and troubled Natalie no more.

Nicholas's phone calls ceased after the third time Natalie hung up without answering, and she told herself she was fiercely glad. She reiterated this to herself constantly like a litany, and eventually was almost able to believe it. But not quite. The letters he wrote she returned unopened, and finally there was nothing. It was over. Maggie would look at her sometimes with compassion showing through her bright gay manner, but Natalie never faltered, retreating behind a shell that was now much more obvious and impregnable. Only Julia and Maggie suspected the unquiet depths that still simmered behind the calm, cheerful exterior Natalie presented to the world. The girl who had surfaced for a brief, vivid period to play Titania was gone, and a prosaic, efficient mortal now functioned in her place.

CHAPTER TWELVE

Six months later Natalie returned to the flat through a
bitterly cold December afternoon, chilled to the bone. It
was Christmas Eve and her offices had closed at
midday. Yielding to Julia's plea, Natalie had agreed to
spend Christmas at home in Arden-under-Hill, though
it would be her first visit home since the fateful June
day when she left for London with what had felt like
the mandatory broken heart of romantic fiction. That
organ had proved to be made of sterner stuff, however,
and after several weeks she had come to terms with life
again, with the help of Julia and Maggie, not to
mention a third staunch ally; her unrelenting pride. If
sometimes, in the private dark hours of night, the latter
had proved to be a comfortless companion, she never
admitted this to anyone, not even herself.

Julia had developed the habit of coming to London
quite regularly at weekends, and the two of them, often
accompanied by Maggie, if she were free, explored
museums and art galleries, saw new films and an
occasional play. On one memorable occasion Natalie
and Maggie even took Julia to a rock concert, though
the latter declared in amusement that at her age, while
glad of the experience, once was more than enough.
Mother and daughter made the proposed visit to Paris
to see Cordelia and Jean-Luc in the autumn to satisfy
themselves that all was well with the mother-to-be, and
otherwise spent quite a lot of time in the little flat just
talking, making up for all the time spent apart in the
past few years.

Julia almost immediately learned that certain subjects
were tabu. One was Natalie's appetite, or lack of it, the
direct result of which was that her tall figure took on a
fragility that was heightened by a new short haircut that
bubbled all over her head, emphasising eyes that now
looked enormous in her markedly thinner face. The

other forbidden subject was Nicholas Marlowe, full stop. Natalie never mentioned him, and refused implacably to listen when at first Julia tried to plead his cause, soon giving up in the face of the polite blank gaze her daughter turned on her at the sound of his name.

When Julia broached the subject of Christmas Natalie felt a wild surge of panic at the mere thought, but eventually quietened her doubts, unwilling to admit she even possessed any, and agreed to go home, to her mother's intense relief. After all, Natalie argued mentally, there would probably be no necessity to see Nicholas at all. Even if she did she was quite confident that her carefully constructed armour was proof against him by this time. Staying in London was hardly a better prospect, as Maggie was on duty over the entire holiday period.

As Natalie climbed the stairs to the flat on Christmas Eve she heard the telephone ringing. She was laden with last-minute shopping, and in frustration she fumbled frantically for her key, but by the time she finally succeeded in opening the door the ringing had stopped. Frowning in vexation, she packed her gaily wrapped packages into a carrier bag, wondering who her caller had been, then carried the bag down to the car with her suitcase. Shivering despite her sheepskin jacket and fur-lined boots, she ran back upstairs to ensure that nothing had been forgotten, gave a final glance round the flat, then locked up and went down to the car. As she reached the bottom of the stairs Natalie thought the phone was ringing somewhere again, but decided it was one of the other tenants' and settled herself in the driver's seat for her journey home.

The sky was leaden grey, and a few flakes of snow were beginning to flutter down before she had even left Chiswick High Street. Edging slowly along the usual two-lane congestion of the first part of the M4, Natalie looked at the forbidding sky with anxiety and switched on the car radio. Eventually there was a motoring flash warning of severe weather moving down from the north, and Natalie delivered up a prayer to St

Christopher that she could manage to get home before it reached Warwickshire.

By the time she reached Oxford it was snowing in deadly earnest, with all traffic slowed to thirty miles an hour. She crawled up the steep hill out of Woodstock with extreme care, and kept her eyes glued to the road, which was fast taking on an appreciable coating of snow, despite the constant stream of traffic passing over it. Keeping doggedly on, she negotiated the steep slippery hill down into Long Compton with her heart in her mouth, the Mini threatening to skid more than once before she reached the bottom, and made her careful way through the village. When she turned off the main Stratford road for the last tortuous ten miles or so to Arden-under-Hill, Natalie began to have real fears about the possibility of getting through. The snowflakes were falling thick and heavy and the windscreen wipers were fighting a losing battle against visibility. On the less populated road the snow was already very thick indeed, and Natalie kept the Mini at a snail's pace, her eyes red and raw with the constant effort of trying to pierce the falling white curtain in front of her.

Natalie almost wept with relief when the lights of Arden-under-Hill finally glowed a dim welcome through the snow, and she drove carefully through the main street, all the shops closed now and everyone safely indoors. She put the little car hopefully at the steep incline up to Hill Cottage, but this proved too much. The wheels spun in the thick snow, the car slewed round in an incontrollable skid, and ended with its bonnet in the hedgerow. Shaken considerably, but otherwise none the worse, Natalie climbed wearily out and pushed the back end of the car off the road, her boots having difficulty in maintaining a foothold on the icy surface.

Good thing it's a small car, she thought thankfully, shivering. She took out her handbag and the large carrier-bag of presents, then locked the car, deciding to return for her suitcase afterwards. She slithered and slipped up the hill, the snow almost instantly coating her yellow crochet beret and sticking to her sheepskin

jacket. Her brown corduroy trousers were immediately
soaking above her boots, and she gasped in the howl of
a wind that was sweeping the snow into great drifts.
Her eyelashes were almost stuck together as the biting
wind blew snow mercilessly into her unprotected face
and the short, but steep, climb seemed like an attempt
on Everest by the time she staggered up the drive of Hill
Cottage, frozen, sodden and absolutely devoid of the
spirit of Christmas.

She was so immersed in her physical misery that as
she skirted the cottage to get in through the kitchen
door at the back, the fact that the house was in
darkness failed to register. A very faint glimmer
through the glass windows of the kitchen finally
brought it home that there was no electricity
functioning in the house, and as she let herself in
through the unlocked kitchen door, after stamping her
boots and shaking herself vigorously outside first, one
solitary candle in a glass-shaded holder was sitting on
the kitchen table.

Natalie dumped her bags on the floor and unzipped
her boots, calling,

'Mother, I finally made it! Yoo-hoo—I'm home! Is
there a fault with the electricity? Where are you?'

Feeling decidedly uneasy at the silence, she picked up
the candle and crept through the rest of the cottage in
her stockinged feet, but there was no sign of her
mother. She stopped for a moment in the bathroom to
take off her wet beret, and quickly rubbed her hair with
a towel, the light of the candle insufficient to see how it
looked, not that she cared much. She went back
downstairs again, shivering in the cold atmosphere,
puzzled by the lack of a fire in the big fireplace in the
sitting-room, even if the central heating was out of
action. Shrugging, she went back to the kitchen and
screamed in fright as a tall figure burst in from outside,
seizing her in his arms, and startling her almost to the
point of cardiac arrest, even though she knew instantly
who was clutching her so frantically.

'Heavens, Natalie, are you all right?' Nick's voice
was rough with anxiety, but Natalie was breathless and

indignant as she pushed him away, her sudden shock at the advent of an almost invisible intruder making her shrewish.

'I *was* all right, until you frightened me out of my wits bursting in like that, not to mention the fact that I'm worried to death about Mother, I'm sodden, frozen and hungry. What's happened to her?'

'Nothing.' His face was invisible in the near-darkness, but his voice sounded harsh with some suppressed emotion. 'I'll explain everything in due course, but first let me get you over to the house before the garden gets completely blocked up.'

'Why?' demanded Natalie suspiciously. 'Surely I can get the fire going in the sitting-room even if there are no lights, and by the time Mother gets back, though where on earth she is on a night like this——'

'She's not coming back for the time being,' he interrupted, 'she's in Paris with Cordelia; the baby's started. Now come on, I have a small emergency generator at Arden House, and you'll be much more comfortable over there. For Pete's sake stop arguing, woman, and get a move on, or we'll be stuck here!'

In the heat of her resentment at being called 'woman' Natalie glared at him hotly, forgetting he could hardly see her, displeasure overriding any constraint she might have felt at meeting Nick again.

'I don't want to come,' she said flatly, folding her arms.

'That's immaterial,' was the uncompromising answer. 'I promised your mother, so you'll come if I have to carry you. Which do you prefer, under your own steam or over my shoulder?'

Huffily Natalie recognised defeat and began struggling into her chilly damp boots again. There seemed little point in wearing the soaking beret, so she pulled on her sheepskin gloves in smouldering silence and prepared to depart.

'Where's your luggage, Natalie?'

'In the car. I couldn't get the Mini up the hill. It skidded into the hedge, so I pushed the back end in line and came up on foot.'

'I saw it,' he said after a strained little silence. 'I thought you'd had an accident. Did you hurt yourself?'

'No,' she said stonily. 'Shall we get on then?'

'Can you manage to get yourself over to Arden House on your own? The path's not too bad—or at least it wasn't an hour ago. I've been down to the village shop to knock them up for any candles they could spare. The forecast is somewhat discouraging, so I thought I'd best be prepared. I saw your car as I came back up the hill. If you'll give me the keys I'll try to move it, or failing that I'll just bring your luggage. How many suitcases?'

'Just one. I'm only here for a couple of days,' said Natalie casually.

'I wouldn't count on it.'

They locked the house behind them and bent into the screaming wind that tore at them. Nick pulled her close to shout in her ear.

'You'd better come with me—I don't think it's a good idea to separate.'

Taking her consent for granted, he secured her arm in an iron grip and they battled down the hill to the little car, which by now was almost snowed in. It was obvious it would have to stay where it was for the time being, and Nick swiftly unlocked the door and took out her suitcase. Instead of retracing their already obliterated footsteps he guided her on down the hill to the main entrance of Arden House and turned into the drive. Here it was comparatively sheltered by the clustering yew trees, and though the snow was just as thick the wind was blowing it mainly to one side of the drive, leaving a narrow space clearer at the other where they could walk in single file.

While they toiled up the winding incline Natalie's head was literally reeling with the emergency that might have sent her mother to France at such short notice, though surely Nick would have said if anything was really seriously wrong with Cordelia. Shivering with cold and fatigue, she meekly let Nick guide her round the back of the house into the large kitchen, which was filled with blessed warmth, and a wonderful savoury smell emanated from the Aga stove. He switched on just one strip light and turned an assessing eye on her. Natalie leaned wearily against the table and rubbed a hand over her wet face, uncaring of the bedraggled figure she must cut. She looked up at Nick in entreaty.

'Tell me why Mother's gone to Paris, please, Nick. Is something seriously wrong with Cordelia?'

He looked down at her with compassion, an odd look of surprise on his face as he stared down into her upturned face.

'No, Natalie, nothing's too terribly wrong; just your niece or nephew making an appearance about a fortnight too early, and Cordelia wanted her mother. Julia knew you'd understand—I have a note for you from her, but only when you've had a hot bath and changed into some dry clothes.'

Natalie was too tired by this time to make any objections to anything once her immediate fears were partly put to rest, and let herself be ushered upstairs to an old-fashioned, comfortable bedroom with a small fire burning behind a wrought-iron guard in the ornamental fireplace.

She turned to Nick gratefully.

'What luxury! Thank you. Perhaps you'd better change your own clothes, you're just as wet.'

He looked down indifferently at his own sheepskin jacket, the dark trousers below it still tucked into the thick white fisherman's socks he'd worn inside his rubber boots.

'A good rub down will do me. Now then, the bathroom's opposite. Ten minutes' soak to get warm, then downstairs for a drink and the casserole Mrs Corby left for me. I put some potatoes to bake in their jackets, and there's a plain old-fashioned rice pudding in the slow oven, so get your skates on—I'm starving!'

Natalie was left alone, vaguely conscious that she should be objecting to a great many things, but at the moment too shattered to bother about what they were. She opened her case and looked for something to wear. The choice was limited, the contents of her case geared to only a three-day stay. Another pair of thick-rib cord trousers in burgundy and a pale pink silk shirt topped by a V-necked cashmere sweater a few shades darker were the warmest combination, and she took them with her into the big bathroom with the enormous porcelain tub which looked long enough to swim in. Running water which was wonderfully hot she slid into the comforting depths, leaning back with her eyes shut to revel in the sheer bliss of being warm again.

She came to with a start at the sound of hammering on the bathroom door.

'Are you all right in there, Natalie?' bellowed Nick. 'I gave you ten minutes nearly half an hour ago!'

'Sorry.' Natalie hauled herself sleepily upright and began soaping herself. 'I must have dozed off. Won't be long.'

'Dinner's ready, so get a move on!'

Not exactly the most gracious of hosts, thought Natalie, amused, then bit her lip. This was really rather an embarrassing sort of situation, come to think of it; a little difficult to know how to comport herself. And as you don't have a young lady's manual of correct behaviour on hand, she thought wryly, get on your bike and let the poor man get at his beloved dinner.

Feeling human again now she was dressed and warm, Natalie paused in the bedroom only long enough for a flick of mascara and a layer of lip-gloss, noting with appreciation the blaze of the cheerful little fire which Nick had obviously made up while she was in the bath. She dragged a hairbrush through the damp clustering short curls and went downstairs to the kitchen, where her host immediately began to ladle out a delectable-smelling oxtail ragoût, rich with dumplings and vegetables. With a polite smile he asked Natalie to bring in the small plates with the jacket potatoes and led the way into the study, where a small coffee-table was laid for two in front of a roaring fire. Natalie was relieved they were not to use the drawing room, at least, as the thought of the last time she was there would hardly have been conducive to her appetite. At least this room had only pleasant associations, but she switched her mind away from the memory of these also, determined to remain impersonal and all of.

'I'm afraid you've forfeited your pre-dinner drink by your extra time in the bath.' Nick poured out two glasses of claret and handed her one. 'Have a glass of wine instead.'

Natalie accepted it gratefully and sank into the old armchair alongside the fire, her plate on her knees, and began to eat with frank enjoyment. Nick did the same while he explained about Julia's headlong departure.

'Cordelia went into hospital suddenly very early this morning, and your brother-in-law rang in a frenzy to ask your mother if she could possibly get herself over to Paris to be with her. Julia rang me, and I practically burned up the lines getting her on the first possible flight to Orly. By great good fortune, and with a lot of persuasion, I managed it, and I drove her down to Heathrow at the crack of dawn. The trouble was that she refused to ring you up that early in case you were startled, so she rang from the airport, but no joy, you must have already left for the office. She intended trying again from Paris.'

Natalie looked across at him in dismay.

'The phone was ringing just as I got back to the flat, but as soon as I unlocked the door it stopped——' she paused in remorse. 'I think it rang again as I was on my way down to the car, but I was eager to get off and didn't go back.'

Nick's mouth twisted in a bitter little smile.

'I knew there was no point in *my* ringing you. Our lines of communication have been disconnected for quite a while.'

'Yes.' Natalie returned his look evenly, then refocussed her attention on her half-eaten meal, but her appetite had vanished and it was impossible to eat any more. She put her plate apologetically on the table.

'That was delicious, Nick, but you were a bit over-generous.'

He looked at the plate pointedly.

'Just a normal helping; what you've eaten would hardly keep a self-respecting sparrow functioning.'

'Don't exaggerate,' she said lightly, and finished her wine.

Nick got up immediately and refilled her glass, looking disturbingly attractive in a rollnecked white Aran sweater and off-white cords, the leaping firelight playing on strong features and highlighting the fair hair which flopped on his forehead untidily as usual. Natalie felt a surprisingly sharp pang to see how thin and haggard he looked, his tan long faded, and there were dark shadows under his eyes. Despite his acid comments on Natalie's appetite, she noticed that his plate was also half full when he piled the used dishes on a tray to take them out. She rose automatically to help, but he waved her back into her chair and she sat staring into the dancing flames until he returned with the coffee tray and two portions of creamy rice pudding.

'You must find room for this,' he said unequivocally, 'or the cook will be mortally wounded.'

Natalie smiled and took the bowl from him, pronouncing the pudding delicious and managing to eat most of it before she put her spoon down.

'There! Mrs Corby can hardly be offended by that, can she?'

He grinned at her disarmingly.

'I made it, not Mrs Corby.'

Taken by surprise, Natalie grinned back at him involuntarily.

'Sneaky! You know I only ate it to please Mrs C.'

'I thought you'd certainly refuse it if you knew I had anything to do with it.' His face sobered, his eyes glittering in the light from the fire, holding hers deliberately. Natalie changed the subject hurriedly.

'I think you said Mother left me a note?'

He went over to the desk to fetch an envelope, handing it over and seeing to the coffee while Natalie had her usual tussle with her mother's handwriting, which was beautiful to look at, but immensely difficult to read.

'Darling,
    I am writing this in a tearing hurry as Jean-Luc rang at five this morning to say Cordy has gone into

early labour, and as I promised to be with her could
I please get the first flight possible, as she wants me.
You will know only too well how much I hate to
desert you, especially at this time, but am confident
you will agree that Cordy's need is the greater for a
little while.

I have left the turkey ready stuffed in the larder,
Christmas pudding alongside in cloth-wrapped basin,
various goodies in biscuit-tins. Rummage. Will ring
whatever time Baby Cassel puts in an appearance.
Wish I could be in two places at once!

Happy Christmas, love to you, darling,
                    Mother.'

Natalie swallowed the lump in her throat and drank
her coffee, blinking the dampness from her eyes.

'Poor Mother,' she said cheerfully, 'if it were possible
she'd have divided herself into two—one half for Cordy
and the other for me.'

'Except that you don't really need her as much as
your sister at this moment.' Nick's eyes were sardonic.

'No,' agreed Natalie carefully, 'I don't. I merely said
Mother feels like that. I wonder how Cordelia is getting
on, poor love—soothing Jean-Luc in the middle of
everything if I know her. He was already in a fever of
anxiety more than two months ago when I saw them
last.'

'It must be hard from the male point of view; to feel
helpless and possibly guilty at the same time.'

'Guilty?'

'He must feel he's directly responsible for the pain his
wife is experiencing.' Nick's voice was wholly reasonable, but something in the expression on his face made
Natalie change the subject at random.

'At least this baby won't have to put up with a
Shakespearean name all its life. Cordelia was born a
couple of weeks after Mother had been to a
performance of *King Lear*.'

Nick topped up her wineglass and poured a second
cup of coffee for them both, raising an eyebrow.

'How did *you* manage to escape?'

'I didn't. Mother saw *The Tempest* nearest to my arrival, but for various reasons Miranda is my second name.'

Silence fell for an appreciable length of time, but Natalie was too tired to feel uncomfortable, despite the knowledge that Nick was watching her intently as she lay back in the chair, mesmerised by the flames.

'You're terribly thin,' he said abruptly, 'and you've cut off all your beautiful hair.'

Natalie smiled defensively.

'I can't do much about the thin bit, but I must defend my hairdo; much more fashionable and practical. Anyway, I was getting a bit past the stage of having all that hair hanging about.'

'I liked it,' he said quietly. 'You were a beautiful Titania.'

'Thank you, but that was all illusion, after all, not something to carry on into every day life.' Natalie moved in her chair so that her face was out of direct light. 'By the way, Mother says there's a turkey ready stuffed in her larder, and a Christmas pud.'

'Correction. The turkey has now transferred to my own larder, and the pudding. When the electricity was cut I fetched all the contents of your mother's freezer and fridge to put into the ones here.'

'You must have had a frantic afternoon!' Natalie grinned ruefully.

'A frantic day, one way and another. I belted down to the airport with your mother, but at least I was lucky enough to be almost back home before the snow really came down in earnest. The culmination of my day was seeing your car in the hedge.' Natalie was fascinated to see him shudder. 'Hence the rather precipitate greeting—I had visions of streaming blood, or at the very least broken bones. My apologies for frightening you.'

'Totally unnecessary; my fault for being such a coward.' She could afford to be magnanimous in retrospect. 'I had such a nightmare of a journey, I was in a jelly of fear all the way from Oxford, and then to find the house dark and empty was too much. I think it was the candlelight, flickering like a horror movie, that was the cause of it all. You could have been anybody!'

'No doubt it made matters worse to discover it was me,' he said grimly.

'No, Nick, of course it didn't. I was highly relieved, believe me. Now what do we do about two turkeys, as I imagine you already had one?'

'Wrong. I had a booking at a hotel. I was supposed to be spending Christmas there.' Nick's face was expressionless.

Natalie felt utterly stricken.

'And now you're stuck here because of me. Oh, Nick, I'm truly sorry; what a nuisance I am!'

'Rubbish. Apart from the fact that I'd never have made it in this weather, what man in his senses would prefer Christmas in a hotel to one spent in such splendid isolation with a beautiful girl?'

After giving some thought to this last Natalie decided to ignore it and rose to her feet. She looked at her watch and smiled politely at him.

'It's well after midnight, Nick, so I think I'll bid you goodnight, and apologise again for all the trouble you've been caused. I'll cook the turkey in the morning.'

He got up slowly and came round the table, standing close enough to make her keenly aware of him physically.

'I'll make sure the Aga keeps going all night,' he said, then he hesitated. 'Merry Christmas, Natalie.'

'Merry Christmas, Nick.' Natalie's voice was very steady, she noted in wonder as a tense little silence stretched between them and he came fractionally closer, his head beginning to bend slowly towards hers.

Suddenly the silence was shattered by the ring of the telephone.

'Thank goodness it's still working!' Nick threw over his shoulder as he dived into the hall with Natalie hard on his heels.

After he'd listened to the caller on the other end of the line for a moment Nick grinned and passed the receiver over to Natalie.

'A very excited Frenchman on the line asking for you.'

Natalie snatched the phone from his hand.

'Jean-Luc, *ici* Natalie.'

'*Bon anniversaire, joyeux Noel*, Tante Natalie.' The voice at the other end of the line was delirious with joy.

'*Tante!*' shrieked Natalie. 'What is it?'

'A little girl, so perfect and lovely, just like her mother!'

The tears were trickling unashamedly down Natalie's cheeks.

'Oh, Jean-Luc, congratulations, how wonderful! How is Cordy?'

'Beautiful and wonderful, as always. She sends her love, as does your *maman*, who will ring you tomorrow—*non*, today!'

'Give them my love, and tell them—oh, Jean-Luc, tell them——' she stopped suddenly, too full for words.

'They will know exactly what you mean, *chérie*.' His voice was very tender. 'My wife says I must tell you our daughter is to be called Natalie Christiane.'

'My goodness,' Natalie tried to laugh, 'I should have thought one was enough!'

'With such a birthday what other names could be more suitable? *Bonsoir, chérie*.'

'*Bonsoir*, Jean-Luc.' Natalie put the phone down in a daze, only just becoming aware that she was leaning against a wool-clad shoulder. Instinctively she turned her face into it and gave way to the thankful tears that overwhelmed her, almost unaware of the arms which closed protectively around her, cradling her against the broad, familiar chest. After a while Nick turned her face up to his and mopped it with a handkerchief, smiling indulgently.

'I presume all this emotion means that the new baby has arrived.'

'I'm sorry, Nick.' Natalie sniffed valiantly. 'I didn't mean to drench you. It's been such an exhausting and—well, unusual sort of day, and I was secretly very worried about Cordelia. All this is just relief. 'I've been very poor company, I'm afraid.'

His arm tightened momentarily before releasing her.

'Never that, Natalie. Now we must have a drink to wet the baby's head; you can't go to bed without celebrating.'

'I'd love a drink,' she said happily, and went back with him to the warm, welcoming study, where Nick added a few coals to the fire. 'As long as it's not vodka.' She pulled a face, but didn't enlarge as he raised an enquiring eyebrow.

'I suppose it should be finest French champagne under the circumstances,' said Nick, surveying the tray of drinks on the desk, 'but I'm afraid I can only run to sherry, extra dry, Scotch or brandy. There's ginger ale for mixer, if that appeals.'

Natalie accepted brandy with ginger ale to mark the arrival of Mademoiselle Cassel, curling up comfortably in the armchair with the clinking glass.

'No doubt this will be the last straw, though. I'll probably be legless!'

'In which case I shall be only too happy to carry you to bed,' began Nick, then stopped short, and there was a pregnant little silence again, which Natalie broke brightly, saying the first thing that came in to her head.

'They've named the baby already. She's to be Natalie Christiane, would you believe!'

Nick looked across at her sharply.

'Is today *your* birthday, too, Natalie?'

'Yes.' It was hardly something she could deny.

'Many happy returns.' With one graceful movement he rose and pulled her to her feet, swiftly kissing her cheek. 'Come along, bedtime, I think. You've had a fairly hair-raising day, one way and another.'

Natalie was too tired to feel any awkwardness as he led her up the cold stairs, and left her at her bedroom door with a brief goodnight. She was barely able to get through the bother of undressing herself before sinking into the comfortable bed in the warm, firelit room, too wearied by all the taxing events of the day to dwell on the unexpected turn of events. Sleep was almost instantaneous, and she was out to the world until a knock on the door next morning brought her back from dreamless depths to the sound of Nick's voice outside.

'Merry Christmas, birthday girl. Sorry to disturb you, Natalie, but I don't know what to do about the turkey and I think it should go in the oven shortly if we're to eat it today.' There was a pause, while she struggled upright, yawning. 'I have a cup of tea in my hand; may I bring it in?'

Natalie called out in the affirmative, and pushed her hand through her ruffled curls, undisturbed at the sight of Nick in workmanlike navy blue sweater and jeans, careless even of the fact that he should see her in her nightgown, which was a high-necked demure affair with frills at throat and wrist. She bade him a sleepy good morning and accepted the cup gratefully, unconscious of her tousled appearance, a fact which only seemed to amuse Nick, who made no move to depart, and stood watching her dispose of the hot tea, as though this were an everyday occurrence.

'Right then,' she said briskly, handing him the mug, 'that was just what I needed. I'll be five minutes—tell the turkey to hang on till then!'

She was as good as her word. Dressed in the now dry brown cords and a high-necked cable-stitch ochre wool sweater, she ran downstairs a few minutes later feeling surprisingly rested, and not in any way put out by the uncharted way her Christmas was turning out. Nick was at the stove, frying what promised to be a very substantial breakfast, and on the counter top alongside him the turkey sat in splendid isolation, awaiting her ministrations. She examined the bird with awe.

'My goodness, how many was Mother intending to feed? That's an absolute monster!'

Nick chuckled, deftly arranging bacon, mushrooms and eggs on two plates.

'She won it in the W.I. raffle.' He pulled out a chair for Natalie and put a laden plate in front of her. 'Eat that before you attack the bird, another few minutes won't make much difference—we're not exactly in a hurry, are we? There's nowhere we can go.'

He jerked his head towards the view from the

windows as he sat down, indicating what little was visible of the garden, which was a foot deep in snow, every tree coated with glistening white in the still clarity of the cold sunlight.

'I was supposed to go back to London the day after tomorrow.' Natalie began to eat hungrily, her appetite unimpaired by what seemed the extreme improbability of the prospect.

'I think you can forget about that. For one thing the Mini won't get any attention for a bit. No one is working today or tomorrow, even if they could get at it—which I very much doubt.' Nick attacked his breakfast with gusto. 'I suppose you might get back by train if it thaws. No doubt you have a lot on socially,' he added casually. He looked at her across the table in a neutral, friendly way that put her completely at ease. For the moment they were as relaxed together as though the events of the past few months had never occurred. Natalie poured out coffee for them both and buttered a piece of toast for herself.

'Nothing that matters in the slightest,' she said cheerfully. 'I was hoping Mother might go back with me, but as she's very much occupied anyway I'll just stay here for a bit—I mean at the cottage when the electricity's back on. By the way, Nick, it's just occurred to me, why did Jean-Luc ring here, instead of to the cottage?'

'I imagine your mother thought you might be here when her phone didn't answer,' he said blandly. 'No doubt she'll be ringing you herself shortly.'

'In which case I'd better deal with our dinner. Any idea what the turkey weighs?' Natalie jumped up and surveyed the bird consideringly.

'Your mother said something in the region of twenty-three pounds, I think.'

Natalie made rapid calculations as to cooking times and decided they would do best to eat it for dinner that evening.

'I don't suppose you have any roasting bags?' she asked hopefully.

Nick stopped short in the middle of clearing away the breakfast things, his face baffled.

'What are they, for heaven's sake?'

'I rather thought you wouldn't. Never mind, I'll cover him with bacon strips and put him in the oven breast down, and that should do it.' Natalie suited her words to action, but Nick picked up the baking tray with the prepared bird and deposited it in the oven.

'Thank goodness Mother stuffed the thing,' said Natalie thankfully. 'I must be honest and admit I've never done that myself.'

'Were you here for Christmas last year?' Nick refilled their coffee cups and they sat down at the table again to enjoy their coffee at leisure.

'Oh yes, I come home for Christmas every year. Cordelia and Jean-Luc were here too, and—and Edward.' She faltered for a moment, then went on resolutely. 'How about you? What do you normally do?'

'Friends usually. This year I opted for a hotel.' Nick's face sobered. 'I felt like anonymity this year, Natalie, for reasons too obvious to mention.'

'Yes,' Natalie had no intention of resuming hostilities, 'but the forces of nature decreed otherwise and here we are, so we'll just have to make the best of it. Come on, I'll wash and you can dry.'

They were determinedly friendly after that, both occupied with preparing all the accompaniments to the dinner. Natalie put the pudding on to steam and made brandy sauce to accompany it, insisting on bread sauce with the turkey, although Nick rather smugly produced a jar of cranberries. Peeling vegetables and making up fires occupied them fully until midday, when Nick called a halt, leading Natalie firmly into the study to drink sherry in front of the huge fire while they listened to Christmas programmes on the transistor radio.

'I suppose you're saving the generator for later—it doesn't appreciate too much of an overload, I presume?' Natalie asked idly, curled up in the shabby velvet armchair.

'No problem, really,' answered Nick, staring into the flames, 'I thought an old-fashioned Christmas to match the snow would be a change. By all means switch on the television if you wish.'

She shook her head emphatically.

'This is much better; television has made conversation almost a lost art.'

They both looked up simultaneously, their eyes locking, both unable to look away until Nick finally said huskily:

'More sherry?'

Natalie nodded wordlessly and held out her glass in a hand not quite steady, feeling relieved when the sound of the telephone galvanised them both into action.

'Mother!' she exclaimed, and ran into the hall, Nick close behind her.

It was indeed Julia, bubbling over with Christmas and birthday wishes and news of the baby, who, of course, was quite the most beautiful child ever to come into the world in the opinion of the hopelessly doting parents. Cordelia was well, and sent loving messages, as did Jean-Luc. Then, after a little pause,

'And you, birthday girl? How are you coping, under the circumstances? I rang through to the cottage, but presumed you'd come over to Nick again when there was no answer.'

'I haven't been home. We're snowed in and the electricity's off. Nick has an emergency generator for light, the turkey is occupying his Aga cooker and we're imbibing Christmas cheer in front of a huge fire.' Natalie was inhibited from enlarging further by the presence of the man lounging against the hall table alongside her. There was a small silence at the other end of the line, which Nick broke, taking the phone from Natalie.

'I'll take great care of your ewe-lamb, Mrs R. No need to worry at all. About anything.' He paused, grinning at Natalie while he listened to the voice coming over the line. 'Yes. Yes, I'll do that.' He handed the phone back to Natalie.

''Bye for now, Natalie. I'll be thinking of you, darling.'

''Bye, Mother. Love to the others.'

Natalie turned to Nick immediately as she replaced the receiver.

'What was she saying to you?'

'Merely telling me that our presents are over at the cottage in the sideboard in the dining room, when we can get over there.'

As they returned to the study, after a quick look at the turkey, Natalie excused herself and went upstairs to her room. She made the bed, trying to decide whether to give Nick the present she'd bought for him impulsively the week before, not knowing whether she'd ever bring herself to the point of handing it over to him. She opened her suitcase and took out the gaily wrapped package kept deliberately separate from the rest in the carrier bag in case her mother would have discovered it by accident.

Natalie held the parcel in her hands for a long time, then made her decision and took it downstairs before she changed her mind. Marching into the study, she said almost militantly,

'I bought you a present. I hope you like it—Happy Christmas.'

Nick stood for what felt like forever, just looking at the parcel in her outstretched hand. Brushing back his hair, he turned a disbelieving look on her finally, with something in his eyes she interpreted as hope before he untied the scarlet ribbons and took off the red and gold striped paper.

'I found it in a second-hand bookshop, covered in dust, and thought it might be useful. I hope you like it,' she said nervously.

The book in his hands was old and battered, a volume of one John Kincaid's *Adventures in the Rifle Brigade*.

'He was actually at Waterloo,' said Natalie.

'I know.' Nick was obviously deeply touched. 'I hardly know what to say. As you can imagine, I never even thought you'd give me anything.'

'Neither did I.' Natalie was honest. 'Even after I'd bought it I didn't know whether I'd ever actually hand it over. I hid it at the bottom of my case and sort of let events decide for me. I hope I haven't embarrassed you.' It suddenly struck her that as he was unlikely to have anything for her in return the book might be rather a mixed blessing. 'Please regard it as a thank-you for your hospitality.'

To her surprise Nick laughed and moved to kiss her cheek very briefly.

'Thank you for such a very thoughtful present, ma'am, and I know perfectly well you think I'm put out because you think I have nothing for you.'

Natalie was relieved, and dimpled pertly at him.

'You're not horrified, then?'

'Not in the least. Because I did buy you something.' He laughed outright as the colour rose in her cheeks and she looked at him in confusion. 'I was going to leave it with your mother if all my original plans had materialised. As it is, I'll chance handing it over in person.'

He went over to the desk and opened the top drawer, taking out a small box embellished with gold ribbon, pushing her down into her chair as he put the box into her hand. Natalie regarded it with misgivings.

'You look like a member of the demolition squad about to defuse a bomb,' Nick teased, refilling her sherry glass. 'Go on, it won't bite you.'

Refusing to look up at him, Natalie unwrapped the present with great care, then opened the small leather box, staying mute and unmoving as she stared at its contents. A small gold heart, set with a turquoise and outlined in seed pearls, lay within, attached to a fine gold chain.

'It's quite, quite lovely,' she said huskily at long last, 'but you shouldn't have given me something so—so——' she trailed into silence, unable to go on.

'Emotive?' he suggested lightly.

'Expensive, actually.' Natalie refused to be drawn. 'I don't know that I can accept it.'

'I hope you will,' he said earnestly. 'The only other person I could give it to is Mrs Corby; hardly her style really, and I bought your mother a Limoges pin-tray.'

'In that case, thank you very much.' Natalie felt there was little else she could say, at the risk of being ungracious, and even went so far as to reach up to kiss his cheek with what she felt was considerable sangfroid. This was a miscalculation. All Nick's determinedly impersonal friendly manner disappeared suddenly and completely and with a suppressed groan of something bordering on anguish he locked his arms round her and turned her face to his, kissing her mouth with the desperation of a man given water after being lost in the desert.

Natalie was too much taken by surprise to resist. Nick slid a hand into her hair, holding her head captive as his mouth moved hungrily over hers, his other arm holding her fast against him. Breathing rapidly, he murmured between kisses, his words unintelligible in the force of the emotion possessing him.

'Darling, darling,' he whispered when eventually he lifted his head, 'I've dreamed, starved, lain awake at night imagining I was doing just this—and this.'

He sat down in the big chair with her body cradled in his arms, his mouth endlessly on hers as his hands crept beneath her sweater and stroked warm skin gently, while she lay passive beneath his touch, bemused by the warmth and the sherry she had consumed and the suddenness of his onslaught. Finally her utter stillness communicated itself to the man through the haze of desire that enveloped him. He raised his head and looked down at the wide dark eyes staring unwaveringly into his.

'You slammed the door in my face.' Her voice was quiet and unemotional.

'Natalie, darling——'

'You turned me out of your house without a fair hearing,' she went on inexplorably. The mist of passion cleared from the grey-green eyes, so close to her own she could make out with clarity the dark rim that circled the irises.

'You slammed the phone down on me,' he returned, controlling himself with an obvious effort, but not relaxing his hold. 'You refused to open my letters.

What could I do but wait, then wait again, hoping that your hurt would lessen? I couldn't get that scene out of my mind, Natalie.' His arms tightened round her even more fiercely. 'That—that apology of a fiancé of yours was actually on top of you! Natalie, you were almost naked beneath him as I came through the door. If I'd stayed I'd have beaten him to a pulp. So I went—and drank myself into oblivion.'

Natalie stirred restlessly in his embrace, which slackened immediately.

'You never tried to see me.' Her voice was almost inaudible.

'Much against my better judgment I followed your mother's advice and left you alone,' he said harshly, 'and greatly though I'm fond of her I think she was utterly wrong. I should have given you a breathing space, then pestered you until you gave in.'

'I think she was wrong, too.' To his surprise and hope she agreed with him.

'Oh, my love——' he began huskily.

'Because you see, Nicholas,' she went on as though he'd said nothing, 'I've rather sorted out my life to do without you. I refuse to think about you, or let Mother talk about you, and frankly I think I feel safer that way. To me, men just spell trouble with a capital T. I don't know that I care to lay myself open to all that misery a third time.'

'You mean first Edward, then me?' His voice was heavy.

'Not quite.' Natalie put his arms away gently and got up from his lap. 'I mean first you, then you again. I don't think I can face a third time. Now I'm going to see what our dinner is doing.'

She went quietly from the room, leaving Nick sitting sprawled in utter deflation, as though something had just winded him. Which it had.

Natalie's calm lasted only as far as the kitchen. She shut the door carefully behind her, trembling suddenly from head to foot. Trying resolutely to pull herself together, she tucked up her sleeves and reached for an ovencloth. Dashing tears impatiently from her eyes, she

opened the oven and drew out the shelf with the heavy
roasting tin and its fragrant-smelling burden. She tilted
the pan slightly to spoon the hot fat and juices over the
bird, her eyes still blurred with tears, when suddenly,
with a rush, the turkey tilted forward on its rack and
the whole tin slid out of her grasp, cascading scalding
hot fat over her exposed wrist. She screamed in agony
and the roasting tin and rack, complete with turkey,
landed on the kitchen floor.

Nick was through the door before she could get to
her feet, taking in the scene at a glance, and dragged her
to the sink, holding her wrist under cold running water
with one hand, his free arm holding her tightly round
the waist.

'The turkey, the turkey!' moaned Natalie, struggling
in his grasp.

'Blast the turkey, I'm more concerned about you,'
Nick said fiercely, noting with anxiety that her face was
completely colourless. 'My darling, please don't faint
for a moment, at least until I've reduced the burn a
little.'

'I'm not going to faint,' said Natalie irritably, 'but
the turkey will spoil——'

'Will you shut up about the turkey! Now, is that a
little better?' Nick withdrew her hand from the water
and sat her down at the table with her arm in a clean
tea-towel. She nodded.

'Please put the turkey back in to cook,' she pleaded,
feeling slightly sick, though the throbbing in her arm
was lessening.

'Oh, for Pete's sake!' exploded Nick, and picked up
the tin, returned the turkey to it and rammed it in the
oven. 'Now; let me look at that arm.'

Natalie was surprised to find the burning sensation
already much lessened.

'It's throbbing still, but it's not hurting unbearably
now,' she said.

Nick knelt alongside her, his arm round her waist,
looking at her with troubled eyes, his fair hair flopping
wildly over his forehead, the scar now practically
unnoticeable.

'It's almost gone,' said Natalie softly.

'What?'

'Your scar.'

'It's your hand that worries me—how is it now?'

'Just smarting a little, that's all. I was lucky.'

'You frightened the hell out of me!'

'I'm sorry.'

'Natalie——' he looked at her in entreaty.

'Yes.'

'Did you mean what you said in the study?'

Natalie was silent for a long time.

'I thought I did.' She smiled sadly. 'You didn't trust me, you see.'

Nick pulled her up by her uninjured hand.

'Let's go back to the other room, and get you over your shock.'

Natalie went, unresisting, letting him install her on the settee, which he pushed nearer the fire. Putting on more coal, he said over his shoulder,

'Have some more sherry.'

'Is that good for burns?' Natalie giggled.

'Good for something,' he grunted, and sat beside her, an arm around her, gently propelling her head down to his shoulder. They sat sipping their drinks for a little, watching the flames curling round the new coals. Eventually Nick took away her glass and put it with his own on the desk behind them, then settled her wholly in his arms, his chin on top of her head.

'It wasn't a case of not trusting,' he said, as though there had been no intermission in the conversation, 'nothing so cerebral, I'm afraid. It was so unexpected and sickening to walk in through a wide open door and see you both there like a scene from some lurid sex film. I saw red—literally. There was a red mist inside my head and I had to get away. No question of trust, just involuntary recoil and a blind instinct to put distance between myself and what was apparently taking place in front of me. I was full of a sick rage that made me behave like a madman, so that I couldn't even listen to you when you came to see me. By the time I was able to think rationally again it was too late. The damage was done. You wouldn't communicate with me and it was all over.'

'The new fiancée had jilted Edward. He got roaring drunk and made instinctively for me, I think initially for comfort,' explained Natalie. 'I was having a shower, hence the lack of clothes, and suddenly he went bananas! I threw him out neck and crop after your dramatic entry and exit, and I've done my level best to erase you both from my life ever since. As far as Edward was concerned I succeeded admirably. Getting over you has been an uphill struggle.'

'Did you succeed?' Nick's deep voice was very soft.

The girl in his arms heaved a great sigh.

'I'd rather not commit myself on that for the moment. Let's just—let things drift and celebrate Christmas, Nick. No more hostility, but I can't veer suddenly from one course to another quite so abruptly. Bear with me a while.' She turned in his arms and smiled up at him. 'I loved the pendant, Nick, thank you very much. I'll treasure it.'

He looked silently into her face for a moment, then, almost as if it were dragged from him, he said slowly,

'I love you so much, Natalie. Whatever else you may think of me, at least please believe that.'

'I'll try.' Natalie smiled in an effort to lighten the atmosphere. 'Now this time you can come with me and wash the kitchen floor where it's probably encrusted in grease. My hand is a great deal better, but I'll use it as a good excuse to get out of the chores!'

From then on the day was spent amicably in preparing the dinner, which they ate eventually by candlelight, with the added pleasure of champagne Nick insisted on opening to accompany the turkey, which despite its misadventures was pronounced perfect. Afterwards they cleared away and washed the dishes, Natalie putting them away while Nick braved the sub-zero temperature outside to bring in a further supply of logs and coal. Then they settled in the study to watch the Christmas film on television, finally switching it off to talk for ages about Nick's book and the considerable

progress made without, as he put it, any distraction to
keep him from his labours.

Natalie had changed for dinner, wearing the one
dress included in her packing, a brown wool crêpe with
a low neckline that displayed Nick's gift perfectly. She
sat in one corner of the settee, her legs in sheer dark
tights drawn up beneath her as she listened intently to
his account of his novel up to its present stage of
completion.

'What's your heroine, Georgiana, like to look at?' she
asked with interest.

'Bronze curls, dark eyes, tall, slender and utterly
enchanting,' said Nick, his voice deepening as he looked
at her with an expression that made her breathless.
'Every man's dream of fair woman, I suppose. Certainly
mine.'

Natalie was silenced, a slight flush along her
cheekbones as she turned away from the intensity of his
eyes which seemed to reach out and touch her as
tangibly as though his fingers were on her skin.

'Natalie,' he breathed, utterly still in his corner of the
sofa, 'I want you so much. Are you totally immune to
the fact that we're alone, no one within a mile of us,
and I love you so much it's sending me insane?'

'It would be a pity if that happened,' she murmured,
looking down at her bandaged wrist with painstaking
attention.

'Are you prepared to help avert such a tragedy?'

'How?'

'Like this.'

Nick slid across the settee and lifted her face to his.
Looking down into it for a long moment, he let out his
breath, then kissed her deeply, holding her close while
he kissed her hair, her eyelids, her freckles, then at last
her parted mouth again. Abruptly and simultaneously
they caught fire, their entire bodies igniting as they
pressed together. Natalie gasped and thrust herself
harder against him as his hands became less gentle and
his kisses more urgent. Breathing rapidly, he swung
round so that they were lying pressed together full
length, her fingers frantic with the buttons of his shirt.

Then her mouth was open and moist against his chest, her tongue tasting him and her teeth fastening on the blond hair, tugging gently, sending great tremors racing through him. He found the zip at the back of her dress and slid it down until the dress fell from her shoulders leaving her breasts protected only by a brief flimsy bra that presented no obstacle to his feverish hands that unfastened and discarded it impatiently to give his lips access to her skin, his tongue teasing first one nipple then the other while she stiffened, gasping, pushing herself convulsively against him as he took each nipple gently between his teeth.

'Natalie, I have to stop now, or I won't be able to,' he muttered hoarsely, his body trembling against her.

'No!' she said through clenched teeth.

'Darling——' he was silenced as she opened her mouth on his until they were both dizzy with desire and conscious of nothing except the overwhelming need flooding them both to the exclusion of all else. Then with a superhuman effort Nick tore his mouth from hers and swung violently away to sit, head in hands, his breath coming in great gasps as he fought for self-control.

Natalie watched him dumbly, the blood thundering along her veins, a deep ache of unfulfilled longing consuming her, then she stood up, fastened her dress and, not daring to touch the man still deep in the throes of his struggle for control, she went noiselessly from the room and up the stairs to her solitary bed, racked with guilt that after all it had not been her decision that she would now occupy it alone.

One way and another, Natalie slept very badly that night, her mind and body tormented with desires that were new and surprising to her. When she woke up after a restless, uneasy sleep, waves of embarrassment swept over her at the prospect of encountering Nick in the cold light of day. The bedroom fire had been banked overnight, and she got out of bed to stir it into life, putting more coal on and hurriedly huddling into her dressing gown as she went over to the window to look out. Snow had fallen again during the night and the garden looked more like an Alpine scene than Warwickshire, every tree heavily laden with snow, which flashed and sparkled like diamonds in the pale icy sunlight of morning. Natalie jumped at the knock on the door, her heart turning over at the sound of Nick's voice, the defensive calm of the past few months apparently lost and gone permanently.

Nick opened the door cautiously and peered round it, then smiled so tenderly when he saw her standing there barefoot, all her qualms seemed suddenly foolish.

'Come on, sleepyhead, get your clothes on and let's go and do some digging. After you've eaten the breakfast I'm cooking, that is.'

Natalie grinned back, all at once completely at ease.

'Yes, sir—I'm starving! Though if I keep on eating all these enormous quantities of food I'll be as fat as a pig.'

Nick eyed her up and down, his mouth lifting in a lopsided smile.

'That danger seems hardly imminent for a while yet, so get a move on—I'm hungry.' He paused a moment in the doorway. 'Did you sleep well, Nat?'

'No, I certainly didn't!'

'Neither did I.' He let out a great sigh, then they both burst into laughter as he left her to get on with dressing.

The laughter set the scene for a day Natalie enjoyed enormously. Nick found an ancient pair of Wellingtons that with the addition of a pair of his socks fitted Natalie reasonably well, and after breakfast they both went outside to clear the paths around the house. The violent exercise gave them both a high colour and enormous appetites, and at lunchtime Natalie opened tins of soup and made thick sandwiches from what looked like being an inexhaustible supply of turkey. During the afternoon Nick battled his way over to Hill Cottage to see that all was well, while Natalie put potatoes to bake in the Aga and made a fricassee of the turkey ready for the evening. Nick came back with two large cake tins, on Natalie's instructions, one containing a Christmas cake, the other full of mince pies, and they made inroads on these before going outside to revert to childhood and build a snowman, until eventually

Natalie yielded to the irresistible temptation of shying a snowball at Nick. The ensuing fight finally drove them indoors, weak with laughter, their outer clothing wet with snow.

'Bathtime, Nicholas,' said Natalie firmly.

'Yes, Nannie,' he mocked, unbuttoning her jacket. 'You first—and don't be long, no falling asleep.'

He dropped a kiss on the tip of her nose, then instantly drew back and pushed her through the door in the direction of the stairs.

Natalie scrubbed herself vigorously in the bath, singing loudly about Rudolph the red-nosed reindeer in her distressingly off-key voice, until Nick thumped on the door.

'Hurry up,' he yelled, 'it's my turn!'

Half an hour later they were once more settled in front of the study fire with plates of steaming food on their laps, eating as though they had fasted all day. Natalie was wearing her brown dress again, and Nick had a suede jacket over a wool shirt instead of the usual sweater.

How attractive he is, thought Natalie, as she watched the firelight playing on his thick, blond hair, the heavy-lidded eyes absorbed as he ate with frank enjoyment, unaware that she was watching him. Eventually he looked up to meet her eyes, a question in his.

'What is it, Nat?'

'Nothing really.' She returned to her dinner. 'I was just thinking what a lovely day it's been.'

He smiled in agreement.

'This is the first real sit-down we've had all day. I believe we've been what's known as channelling one's energies. In other words, I thought that by being occupied all the time I might just possibly succeed in keeping my hands off you.'

To his delight Natalie flushed scarlet.

'Honestly, Nick, you can hardly have been turned on by woollen mitts and those decrepit wellies!'

'My angel, as I knew what was inside them, what earthly difference did you think that would make?' he demanded, putting his empty plate back on the tray.

'You could turn me on whatever you were dressed, or not dressed, in. Hence all the desperate activity. Are you worn out?'

She shook her head, dimpling at him in a rueful smile. He groaned.

'I'm not in the least tired, either. What shall we do after dinner?'

'Games,' she said decisively, holding up a dismissive hand at the leer on his face. 'Scrabble, or something—anything you can find.'

Nick's search produced playing cards and draughts, and they occupied themselves very diligently with them all evening, studiedly avoiding any contact or look that could spark off the fire that all too evidently lay barely dormant below the surface in both of them. When they finally called it a day it was almost ten-thirty and they both sat chatting desultorily about the new arrival, carefully staying either side of the fireplace until Natalie jumped up and went off to make coffee while Nick banked up the fires. When she came back with two steaming mugs, Nick had a brandy bottle in his hand, and poured a generous amount into each. She raised a doubtful eyebrow at him.

'Help us—me—sleep, I hope,' he muttered, not meeting her eye. There was a tension between them now it was hopeless trying to ignore, and Natalie sat on the rug in front of the fire, cupping her mug between her hands, deeply conscious of the taut figure on the sofa, swallowing down scalding coffee as though it were a cold drink. Nick put down the mug restlessly and turned to look down at Natalie at the precise moment her own eyes turned up to his. Her stomach muscles contracted sharply as they both stared at each other, silent and tense, the laughter all gone. Nick's light eyes were completely dark with emotion, something in Natalie's making him lean forward slowly and take the mug from her hand, setting it on the hearth with infinite care, never taking his eyes away for an instant. She watched, motionless, while he shrugged out of his jacket, letting it slide carelessly behind the sofa, then unresisting she surrendered to the hands that gently drew her upwards until she was standing between his thighs looking down into his face. Still they were silent, then he said softly,

'Natalie, I think you should go to bed.'

'Yes.' Her answering whisper was almost inaudible, her eyes drowsy with an expression that made his mouth dry and blood hammer in his temples. She pulled away from him and stepped back to stand straight and erect, her body outlined by the firelight behind her, eyes wide, with flames dancing in them as she stared down at the man who sat perfectly still in a paralysis of desire. To Nick's utter consternation Natalie went abruptly to the door, turning to look at him over her shoulder, a smile of pure invitation curving her mouth.

'I'm going to bed now, Nick,' she said casually, 'I leave it to you whether you join me there or not.'

His iron control snapped, and with something like a growl he sprang after her, picking her up and carrying her swiftly up the wide cold staircase to the warmth of her firelit bedroom. Driven far beyond the bounds of his control, he jerked back the covers and laid her on the bed, stripping off her clothes and then his own in frenzied haste, and got in beside her, kissing every curve and hollow of her body from head to toe before he was engulfed in such an irreversible tide of desire that nothing on earth could have kept him from possessing the responsive body beneath him that met his every demand with a tempestuous ardour that elated him and elevated both of them to somewhere beyond the stars that glittered frostily in the dark sky outside.

For a long, silent interval they lay entwined, motionless, slowly coming back to a more normal plane where Nick began to feel the cold prodding fingers of remorse. He drew the covers more closely round them, sighing.

'Darling, I'm sorry. I didn't mean all that to happen. Did I hurt you?'

'I suppose you did, a bit—not much. My attention was rather distracted by all the other things I was feeling. When you lose your cool you certainly lose it, don't you?' Natalie turned her head and smiled at him. 'Don't be sorry. I'm not.'

Nick took her flushed, drowsy-eyed face between his hands and looked down at her lovingly.

'You rather clinched the matter yourself, in the end, young woman, you can't throw out that sort of challenge to a man and expect to emerge unscathed.'

'I didn't expect, or want, to be unscathed! I suddenly felt the time was over for shilly-shallying about. Besides, I'd like a baby like Cordelia's, too.'

His face went rigid with shock.

'Oh no! I'll dig us out tomorrow and we'll see the Vicar. I'll get a special licence and bring your mother home from France and we'll get married next week. . . .'

'Hold on!' Natalie laughed up at him, her face aglow. 'Another couple of weeks won't make that much difference. I want Cordy and Jean-Luc here too.'

'How will I survive that long?' said Nick in desperation, 'I want you here with me always, night and day, and no nonsense about working your notice this time—I'm not letting you out of my sight!'

Natalie stretched luxuriously.

'Anything you say, boss. Now cuddle me a bit before we go to sleep.'

Nick looked astounded.

'Do you mean you want me to sleep with you?'

'Yes, please.'

'But, Natalie—I'm only human. I—I won't want just to cuddle you. Already I—I——'

'Want to make love to me again?' she said simply. 'That's good.'

His answer was lost against her mouth and the whole beautiful, inexorable process began again, but more slowly and with less frantic haste this time.

'Don't forget I'm a mere beginner,' she murmured into his throat, 'you can't expect me to be proficient straight away.'

'Then heaven help me when you are!' He crushed her to him until she gasped in protest and his hold slackened sufficiently to allow her slender body its own hesitant seduction of his, to his almost insupportable delight.

Long afterwards she lay close in his arms, their limbs tangled together, reluctant to sleep and lose the magic of their first night together. She wriggled even closer and whispered in his ear.

'Lovely snow, to cut off the electricity. Such a good thing I had to come and stay with you.' She felt Nick's body shake against hers and raised herself to look down into his face, which was just visible in the dying light of the fire.

'What's so exquisitely amusing?' she demanded.

'The snow didn't cut off the electricity. I did,' he confessed.

Natalie shot bolt upright.

'What! Do you mean—there is actually electricity on at the cottage?'

'I switched it off at the mains so that you'd be forced to come home with me.' His face was alight with laughter, though his eyes were just a shade apprehensive.

'You devious devil, Nick Marlowe! Do you mean to say you carted everything over from Mother's just to make the whole thing look authentic?'

'Oh yes. I would have done a great deal more than that, anything in the world to make you spend Christmas with me, Natalie—anything I could, fair means or foul. I intended to have you back in any way possible.'

Natalie stared down at him wide-eyed.

'You really succeeded too, you rotter, didn't you?'

Nick pulled her down to him and held her close.

'This part of it I didn't plan, my lovely. Never in my wildest dreams did I imagine being here with you like this. I didn't dare. My intention was merely to get us back on speaking terms again.'

'I suppose I should be outraged and affronted, or something.' Natalie's voice was muffled.

'Are you?'

'No. I love being a fallen woman, actually—I had no idea how addictive it would be.'

'You will be very legal and respectable as soon as humanly possible, never fear, Natalie Ross. I want that

ring on your finger before you try to escape me again.'
He shook her fiercely. 'Do you hear me?'

'Yes, yes, I hear you. Stop it! I don't want to escape.
If this is prison I like it.' She was serious for a moment.
'I love you, Nick. But I do have just one further
request, though.'

'Anything at all, my darling.'

'As I'm such a novice, I wondered if you would care
to assist me further in my efforts at research?'

Natalie received no answer to this, nor did she really
expect one, as Nick said nothing more at all for quite
some time, but proceeded in other ways, and with
infinite loving care, to show how deliriously happy he
was to further her education as much as she wished, to
their mutual joy and fulfilment.

BOEUF BOURGUINON
(BEEF BURGUNDY)

When Natalie prepares Boeuf Bourguinon for Edward, she is not just making stew. Boeuf Bourguinon is a rich and flavorful method of serving beef and vegetables that requires just a little more effort than traditional stew — but the result is deliciously worth it!

What you need (to serve 6):

- 2 lbs. lean stewing beef, cut into 1½ in. cubes
- 2 tbsp. bacon drippings
- 1 medium cooking onion, chopped
- 1 clove garlic, minced
- 1½ tbsp. flour
- 1½ cups dry red wine
- 1 cup beef stock or bouillon
- 1 tsp. thyme
- 1 tsp. salt
- fresh-ground pepper
- ½ lb. carrots, peeled and sliced
- 10-12 whole small onions
- ½ lb. fresh whole mushrooms
- 1 tbsp. butter
- 2 tbsp. fresh chopped parsley

What to do:

Marinate beef overnight in wine. Reserving wine, brown beef in drippings in dutch oven or stew pot. Remove beef. Add cooking onion and garlic and sauté. Return meat to pot and sprinkle with flour. Add wine, beef stock, thyme, salt and pepper. Bring to boil, then partially cover and simmer for 2-3 hours, or until meat is tender.

About 45 minutes before serving, add carrots and small onions. In a frying pan, sauté mushrooms in butter. Add to stew pot about 10 minutes before serving. Spoon the stew into individual serving bowls and sprinkle with parsley. Serve with crusty French bread and green salad for a hearty delicious meal.

4 FREE

Harlequin Romances

Get all the latest books before they're sold out!

As a Harlequin subscriber you actually receive your personal copies of the latest Romances immediately after they come off the press, so you're sure of getting all 6 each month.

Cancel your subscription whenever you wish!

You don't have to buy any minimum number of books. Whenever you decide to stop your subscription just let us know and we'll cancel all further shipments.